# FORBIDDEN DESIRE

## BY

## *Teresa Gabelman*

# ACKNOWLEDGEMENTS

Donna Bossert, where to start. Thank you so much for everything you do. I seriously don't know how I've gotten along without you before now. Your devotion to finding sexy cover models as well as keeping me on track is inspiring and well appreciated. You do so much and I thank you for all you do. One day we will meet and that will be one of my favorite days....ever!

Warriorettes, what can I say, you ROCK! Thank you for every share, for having my back and know that I take none of it for granted. You are by far the best street team an author could ever have and the drive-bys are the best!

To my ARC team. You have no clue how much it means to me that you take time out of your busy lives to read unedited stories from me. I know for a lot of you that unedited part drives you nuts, but the opinions of how the storyline is going is priceless to me. I know what I am trying to say in a story, but because of you I now know if what I am trying to say is actually being understood. My brain is a very scary place as you all know.

Becky Johnson, the best editor in the world, yes....the whole wide world, thank you for everything. Editor you may be, but a wonderful friend is what I will always call you. I know I can hop on my messages and Becky will be there to talk me down from wanting to throw my computer against the wall. Hot Tree Editing Team.....THANK YOU!

To my family, thank you for the encouragement, the understanding of my tears at times, the craziness that is my life at deadlines and just for having my back always. With you all by my side I can do anything, without you it wouldn't be worth it.

I saved the best for last. The readers, my friends. I will remember always the very first book, Damon, that was sold on Amazon. I don't know who bought it, but I thank them. And then the second, the third and so on, I thank you also. You are the reason I do what I do. Your support means so much and keeps me going. I hope I can continue to bring you my best and please know that is and will always be my goal.

Lee County Wolves

Forbidden Desire

Gabelman, Teresa (2017-4-18). Forbidden Desire (Lee County Wolves Series) Book #3

Kindle Edition.

Editor: Hot Tree Editing

Photo: IStock Photo

Cover Art: Indie Digital Publishing

# Chapter 1

Marcus Foster stood on his brother's porch, arms crossed, leaning against the railing. His eyes were focused on the work crew hired to rebuild the feed mill that had burned to the ground. Rocky's Bar and Grill was just now in the last stages of cleanup, so almost ready for reconstruction. Due to the deaths from the fire, there'd been the necessary investigation, which had inevitably slowed the rebuild down. His eyes found Roxy Patel and a low growl rumbled deep in his chest. She was a beautiful woman and she was his, not that he had openly claimed her. But he knew, his wolf knew that she belonged to him, and his wolf was ready to let the construction workers know it.

"Why don't you just shift, go piss on her leg, and claim her already," Hunter said as he climbed the steps.

"Fuck you, Hunter." Marcus sneered without looking at his younger brother. No, his eyes followed Roxy and Clare as they made their way from the small coffee shop carrying pots of coffee and doughnuts for the workers. The men actually stopped what they were doing, dropped whatever they were holding, and rushed to help Roxy.

"You know—" Hunter began, his eyebrow cocked, but Marcus stopped him.

"No, and I don't want to fucking know," Marcus hissed, then stepped away from the railing when one of the workers touched Roxy on the shoulder, making her flinch.

"Don't do it." Hunter's tone was full of warning.

Marcus's body started to shake, but he kept his wolf at bay, for now. "Then he best remove his hand from her body."

"Why don't you claim her, bro?" Hunter shook his head in frustration.

Relaxing slightly as the man removed his hand, Marcus looked at Hunter. "Because she's still married." Marcus heard the anger in his own voice. He had tried his best to get her to go on a date with him, but that was always her answer. She was still married.

"Okay, well let's kill the son of a bitch and then she won't be married anymore." Hunter shrugged. "Easy fix."

It didn't matter what kind of mood Marcus was in, Hunter always found a way to make him smile. Even though this smile was evil and thoughtful, it was still a smile and took his mind off killing about twenty construction workers. "Yeah, if only." He gave a snort. "Don't think I haven't thought about it."

"We just couldn't let Garrett know." Hunter kept going. "You know how he is about that stuff, but I bet if Janna had a husband who wouldn't sign the divorce papers, he'd be threatening or killing the guy."

Marcus looked to where Roxy was heading back to the coffee shop. All eyes were on her ass as she walked away. Emily had walked from around the corner talking to one of the construction workers, pointing at different things. He noticed that the man looked nervous as did the rest of the men when she appeared. Suddenly, all eyes were staring their way, directly at Hunter, before they fell all over themselves getting back to work. Glancing at Hunter, he saw the satisfied look on his face.

"You shifted in front of them," Marcus said, his eyes narrowing before he laughed. There was no other explanation for the way the workers reacted to Emily.

"Damn straight I did." Hunter nodded. "Those fuckers know exactly who and what my mate belongs to."

"Did you piss on her leg?" Marcus threw out as Hunter started walking away.

"Didn't have to," Hunter tossed over his shoulder as he headed toward Emily. "Just seeing my wolf was warning enough."

Marcus's smile faded quickly as he watched Hunter head to Emily, wrapping his arm around her. "Lucky bastard," Marcus cursed, then looked toward the coffee shop. Roxy was stopped just inside her door, her eyes watching Hunter and Emily before she slowly glanced his way. They stood motionless, staring at each other until she finally looked away and closed the door. What gave him hope was she looked as miserable as he was. Yeah, that shit was going to change.

****** 

"When are you going to put that man out of his misery?" Clare asked, walking around the counter. "Better question, when are you going to put yourself out of misery? And don't ask me what I'm talking about. You know very well what and who I'm talking about."

It was funny how well Clare knew her because that was exactly what Roxy was about to ask, even though Clare was right: she did know. It would have been just to divert the conversation. "I'm married." She answered the same way she always did.

"Kentucky is a no-fault state." Clare had a new comeback for Roxy's go-to answer.

"Meaning?" Roxy frowned, wiping the counter.

"Meaning, that since Kentucky is a no-fault state, you can start dating at any point in the process." Clare grinned. "Meaning, you can get your hands on that good-looking man who was staring you down and looking like he wanted to kill any construction guy who was glancing your way. *Meaning*, you can finally be happy, Roxy."

Roxy had stopped scrubbing the already clean countertop. "And how did you find this out?"

"The great Google. How else?" Clare replied proudly. "It also means just because the asshole has refused to sign and doesn't want the divorce, it doesn't matter. As a no-fault state, the court is required to enter a decree even if only one spouse desires the divorce."

A glimmer of hope filled her chest but vanished quickly. "I don't know, Clare. It can't be that easy." She reminded herself not to get her hopes up. "Nothing with Bruce is that easy."

"Yeah, well that SOB can't change the laws and that is the law." Clare started more coffee. "You need to get a lawyer, Roxy."

"I can't afford a lawyer." Roxy snorted, taking dirty cups to the back to be washed. "It's taking every penny I make to pay Garrett the rent for this place." Roxy was never late with her rent. Not only was it cheap, but Garrett had set everything up and just handed it to her for a place to work, to be involved with their town, and she made damn sure she paid him.

Once in the back, Roxy set the cups in the sink, then leaned against the wall, closing her eyes while trying to stop the shaking in her hands. Just the thoughts of her ex were enough to send her nerves into overdrive. If it hadn't been for Garrett, Bruce would have killed her. She slowly opened her eyes and stared into the sink at the dirty coffee cups, and suddenly, memories came flooding back.

Her ex was not only a control freak, but a clean freak, meaning he expected everything to be spotless, with nothing out of place. Even the silverware needed to be placed in a certain manner. It was exhausting trying to keep up with his expectations, which she never met.

They'd had a whirlwind romance. He'd been charming and caring at first, showering her with everything a woman could ever ask for. And now she knew why. It wasn't until after they were married that she noticed his weird quirks, his short temper, and his true feelings toward her. He loved her, sure, but it wasn't the kind of love she ever wanted to experience again. Yeah, she had fallen into a trap that until her near-death at his hands, she felt she would never escape from.

Something brought her out of her memories, and she was glad for it. She hated remembering how weak she had been during her time with Bruce. If it hadn't been for Garrett Foster, she would probably still be in that situation or dead.

With a sigh, she headed back out to the front. "If the sheriff couldn't deliver the divorce papers to him, then I doubt anyone else can."

"I'll do it." Marcus's deep voice filled the small building.

"And on that note…." Clare grabbed her bag and headed out the door. "Toots!"

Roxy glared at Clare, then glanced at Marcus. "You want some coffee?"

Giving her a narrowed look, he nodded. "And then you can get me those divorce papers."

"He won't sign," Roxy said, pouring a steaming cup for Marcus. Her hand shook, and she wasn't the only one who noticed. She tried to calm her nerves, but it was no use. Whenever Marcus Foster was near, her body responded in ways that not only frightened her but shocked her. She thought after Bruce, no man would ever hold her interest, that her yearning for love would be buried deep and yet, every single time Marcus was around, she felt all of that and more.

Marcus took the pot from her and set it down. "Oh, he will sign." Marcus's body was close to hers as he leaned over her to put the pot back on the burner, his eyes never leaving hers.

Being pressed up against the counter was something Roxy thought would frighten her, but it didn't. She felt no threat from this man, never had. What she did feel was an overwhelming need to crawl up his body and hold on tight, but she would never do that. Would she? "This isn't your problem, Marcus."

A smirk tipped his lips. "Oh, it is my problem." He leaned slightly closer. "Because that son of a bitch is preventing me from doing what I want to do."

Her heart beat so fast she knew he could hear it, and as close as they were, she didn't doubt he could feel it. She licked her dry lips. "And what is that?" she managed to say.

His head tilted as he moved so his lips were only inches from hers. "Make you mine," he replied without hesitation. With his eyebrow cocked, he bypassed her mouth to kiss her on the cheek and then moved away as soon as the door opened.

"Hey, is the cake ready?" Leda's voice broke through to her brain that was racing with Marcus's words, but her eyes refused to leave him as he picked up his coffee and sat down at one of the tables, his eyes remaining fixed on her.

"Yes." She finally managed to answer Leda's question. "I'll get it."

Pulling her eyes from Marcus, she turned and went into the back. Reaching the table, which the cake sat on, she placed both hands on the wooden top, bowed her head and took deep breaths trying to calm her heart. Why couldn't she have met Marcus before Bruce? Why was her life always so messed up? Why couldn't she be brave? Her eyes moved to the dirty frosting knife lying on the table next to the cake, and her stomach clenched. She forcibly had to stop herself from reaching for the knife in a panic to clean it and put it away. Habits were hard to break. Habits born out of fear were nearly impossible to deny.

It took everything she possessed to grab the cake and turn her back on the dirty frosting knife, but she did it. Nausea burned her throat, but still, she did it. She would break her habits before they broke her. Bruce would not win, not anymore. It was her time to be the winner in her life. She was worthy of happiness. As she walked out with the cake, her eyes once again met Marcus's gaze. He sat where she left him listening to Leda excitedly talk about the baby shower happening in an hour. It was at that moment she realized Marcus Foster would definitely be part of her journey toward happiness.

"It's beautiful, Roxy." Leda clapped her hands excitedly as she looked down at the baby cake.

"Thanks." Roxy smiled proudly. She loved baking and really outdid herself with the cake for Janna. It was a round double-tiered white fondant cake with a large blue bow to connect the cakes and a pink baby carriage on the top. She went with pink, blue, and white since they didn't know the sex of the babies yet, or at least they weren't telling anyone. One tier was chocolate and one a buttercream. "I love baking. I've always wanted to decorate cakes, but—"

What the hell was she doing? This wasn't the time for an open discussion on why she had never pursued a passion. Clearing her throat, she handed the cake carefully to Leda.

"Aren't you coming?" Leda frowned, taking the cake.

This was the part that Roxy hated. "I don't think so," Roxy replied, glancing away before pulling her gaze back. "I have some things to take care of, but please let me know if there's anything else you guys need."

"Are you sure?" Leda frowned, sounding disappointed. "I mean, I can help you with whatever you need after the party so you can come," Leda suggested. "Janna really wants you there."

"I'll see." Roxy forced a smile. "Now you better get over there. The party's getting ready to start without the cake."

"Oh crap!" Leda headed toward the door and thanked Marcus who opened it for her. "Please try to come, Roxy. Janna would want you there."

Roxy smiled but didn't say anything as Marcus closed the door and turned toward her. "I need to lock up." She hoped he took the hint because she needed a moment to obsess over what he had said to her before Leda came in the door.

Instead of doing what most would do and leave, he locked the door with a loud click.

"Why aren't you going to the shower?" He cocked his eyebrow.

"I just don't—"

"Don't lie to me, Roxy." Marcus frowned, his eyes watching her closely.

She had to lie because there was no way she could tell him the embarrassing truth. "Marcus, I really need to clean up." She turned and headed toward the back, leaving him standing alone.

Leaving the dirty frosting knife on the table just to prove to herself she could, she went to the sink to do the few dishes she had left. She knew when he walked in. It was as if his very presence surrounded her. She felt safe and that scared her. As weird as that was, he terrified her, or rather her feelings for him did.

He stood close behind her, his heat to her back, and she tried her hardest to ignore him. There was no ignoring Marcus though.

"Janna's going to be disappointed that you aren't there," Marcus said from behind her, his breath brushing through her hair. "Come on, the whole town's going to be there."

Roxy knew all this, but she also knew that they would all have gifts and she wouldn't. "So, I won't be missed," she replied, realizing she had run out of dirty dishes and needed to turn to face him in order to get the frosting knife she'd purposely left on the table behind him.

"Yes, you will," Marcus pressed, not letting it go.

Turning, she went to go around him, but he blocked her way. "Excuse me."

"You going to come?" He didn't budge.

Knowing he wasn't going to let it go, she sighed in defeat. "I don't have a gift." She glanced up at him. "I ordered it, but it still hasn't come in. I can't show up without a gift."

He quickly grabbed her hand, pulling her out from the back. She glanced at the knife, her heart beating erratically. "Marcus, stop. I have to finish cleaning up."

Marcus did stop, but he didn't let go. "Do you want to go?"

"Yes, but—"

"You will have a gift for her." Marcus turned and continued toward the door. "You need anything before we lock up?"

"I need to finish." She looked behind her toward the back room. "I have to clean the frosting knife."

Marcus looked down at her, his eyes darkening. "Fuck the knife, Roxy." His voice was even and low. "The knife can wait. And I know that you haven't left this town since the day you arrived. You order everything online. That bastard and what he did to you will be erased from your memory very soon."

"How did you know?" Roxy whispered, horrified. "No one should know."

"The man who claims you should know." Marcus tilted her chin up when her eyes shied away from him. "And I'm the man who will right your world once and for all."

# Chapter 2

Marcus had to keep his anger in check as he led Roxy toward Garrett's. He felt the tremble in her hand, and it pissed him off that he couldn't do anything at the moment to ease her fear. It was getting cooler out, but today was one of those days that it was warmer. Mother Nature always liked to tease them with warm days before the bitter cold hit.

He gave her hand a squeeze as they stepped up to the porch and then into the house. Emily had decided it was going to be a boy/girl shower. Most of the town was invited, and thankfully, it was a nice day out so most of the party could happen outdoors. He knew Garrett already had the grill burning because he could smell it.

Before they made their way into the kitchen, Roxy hesitated. Stopping, he stared down at her. "You're part of this town, Roxy. You're a part of all of this." He kept his voice low so only she could hear. "Enjoy yourself."

When she didn't say anything, he pulled her into the kitchen, which was activity central.

"It's about damn time," Hunter said to Marcus, but smiled at Roxy. "He's always trying to get out of work."

"No, I'm always picking up your slack." Marcus corrected him, walking over to hug Janna. "And how are you today?"

"Fat." Janna hugged him back.

"You're gorgeous." Marcus patted her stomach.

"Get your hands off my woman." Garrett walked in, threatening him with the spatula he held.

Janna grinned then reached out to Roxy. "I was so disappointed when Leda said you weren't coming. I'm glad you changed your mind."

"So am I," Roxy admitted with a smile. "Now, what can I do to help?"

Emily walked in at that moment. "Can you whip up your deviled eggs?" Emily asked with pleading eyes. "We already have the eggs boiled."

"Absolutely." Roxy nodded, heading straight toward where the eggs lay cooling.

"Is there a recipe for those that you can add chocolate syrup to?" Janna asked with a hopeful frown.

"Oh God, no!" Hunter vehemently shook his head. "Please say no, Roxy."

"Guess there is a way," Roxy said thoughtfully, ignoring Hunter's gagging.

"Dammit." Hunter went to grab the chocolate syrup that wasn't far from Janna, but Janna was too quick and snatched it.

"Touch my chocolate and die." She growled at him, even showed some teeth.

"I'll make some special for you, Janna." Roxy laughed at the relief on Hunter's face.

"And the rest normal for us ordinary unpregnant people?" Hunter's voice whispered, but was loud enough for everyone to hear.

"Janna can have whatever the hell she wants," Garrett warned, his eyes narrowing. "If she wants chocolate deviled eggs, she will get chocolate deviled eggs."

"Dude, are you listening to yourself?" Hunter grouched at his brother who walked outside. "Seriously, have you witnessed the grossness of her pouring that chocolate syrup on shit that chocolate syrup doesn't belong on and eating it? She damn near made me puke when she poured that shit on her scrambled eggs. I ran out of the house like a little bitch."

Janna grinned. "You did look like a bitch."

Marcus heard everything that was said, but the smile on his face was from the satisfaction of watching Roxy relax and laugh at his dumbass brother. She was beautiful. She was sweet, cared for people and their feelings. She had a quiet strength that drew him to her. She was the kind of woman a man could walk in the door after a long day, and the weight of the world would drop from his shoulders because she was waiting. He had never been attracted to women with red hair. He had always been a blonde kind of guy, but Roxy Patel had changed that the day she had come into town.

From the moment he saw her, he'd known she was his mate. When his brother had told him about how he'd witnessed her humiliation at the hands of her husband, it had sent Marcus into a killing rage. It took Garrett tackling him to get his rage under control. That alone told him she was his mate. And he knew his brother had held back a lot of the story, though he'd heard enough to know she had been treated badly. Hell, he had seen her bruised face, something he would never forget. Roxy had been a stranger to him, yet learning about the danger she'd been in had his wolf tearing to break free.

"You're starting to creep people out." Hunter's voice broke through his thoughts.

"What?" Marcus took his eyes off Roxy to look at Hunter.

"Seriously, you had a crazy stalker look in your eyes." Hunter shivered, trying to hide a grin.

"You love pissing me off, don't you?" Marcus growled, not really caring he'd been caught staring at Roxy. Maybe it was stalkerish, but he didn't give a shit.

"Yes." Hunter thought for a minute. "Yes, I do."

"You're an asshole," Marcus shot back then headed toward the back door.

"Yes." Hunter followed him. "Yes, I am."

Marcus ignored him as he looked over the yard. People were arriving, enjoying the unusually warm day and catching up with neighbors and friends. This town needed a party after what had happened weeks earlier. Since a rival pack had arrived looking for trouble and trying to take control, no one else had shown up to challenge their alpha, Garrett. After killing Darnell Waters, their pack had left a young wolf alive to spread the word, and no one fucked with the Lee County Wolves; they were here to stay.

The town was still on edge, never letting their guard down. Everyone could sense it, but until the town was rebuilt from the fires, it would be that way. Marcus headed toward Garrett who manned the grill, his eyes landing on the rebuilding of the feed mill before traveling toward where Rocky's Bar and Grill had stood.

"Guess they're ready to start rebuilding," Marcus said, seeing a new construction crew setting up as trucks with supplies rolled into town.

"Yeah, I sent Dell over to help Liz." Garrett slapped some more hamburgers on the grill. "I talked her into rebuilding. She just wanted to let it go, said without Rocky, it wasn't worth it."

Marcus nodded, his eyes still staring toward the empty lot that had been bulldozed clean. Liz and Rocky were wonderful people, but with Rocky's death a year earlier, Liz seemed to be going downhill fast. He understood Garrett's reasoning of having her keep busy. She was only in her early sixties, but Rocky's death had aged her.

"You're a good alpha, Garrett." Marcus gave him a nod.

"And one hell of a griller." Hunter came over, grabbing a hot dog. "Is this shit ready yet? I'm starving."

"Will you stop eating and help me?" Emily pinched Hunter on the ribs. "I swear you eat more than anyone I've ever known."

"I'm insatiable." He gave her a wink. She blushed then rolled her eyes.

"Set up more chairs please." Emily sighed but gave him a hug before a loud bang made her jump.

Everyone looked toward Rocky's to see them unloading lumber.

"I'm so glad Liz is rebuilding." Emily smiled excitedly.

"So am I." Hunter grinned before grabbing another hot dog. "Rocky's has the best chili in Kentucky."

Marcus shook his head as he headed to get more chairs. Hunter was a good man, but he could drive a saint insane.

"Hey, Marcus." Linda Cadel stepped up and walked with him.

"Linda." Marcus smiled down at her. He knew she felt something for him, but he had never encouraged her and couldn't find it in himself to be mean. He just wasn't interested. "Glad you could come."

"I wouldn't have missed it," Linda replied. Her stare was an invitation, and he knew it. "Maybe you could walk me home afterward."

And that was exactly why he was put off by most women. He didn't like to be chased. Some men might like it, but not him. He was the chaser. Roxy had just walked outside, her hands full with deviled eggs. Okay, maybe he needed to rethink that. If Roxy Patel was the woman chasing him, he could and most definitely would tolerate that.

"I'll make sure someone gets you home, Linda." Marcus really tried not to hurt the woman's feelings, but he wasn't into playing games either. "Enjoy the party."

He headed toward Roxy and took the heavy plate from her. "Please tell me you kept the chocolate ones separate." He grinned, then grimaced. Hunter was right; that was some disgusting shit.

"I did." She laughed with a nod. "Janna has already eaten most of them."

"Glad I missed that." Marcus sat the plate on the table filled with food. The wind picked up, her scent filling his senses. Damn, she smelled good.

"Actually, it wasn't that bad." Roxy grinned at his expression of disgust.

"You ate one?"

"I always taste what I cook before serving it to anyone." Roxy shrugged. "And it wasn't bad."

Marcus stared at her for a long second. "You're lying."

"I am not." Roxy's shocked expression was obviously fake. "I saved one for you and Hunter."

"Saved me one what?" Hunter asked as he walked up, eyeing the deviled eggs, his arm wrapped around Emily.

"A deviled egg," Roxy replied, setting the smaller plate down in front of him. "Go ahead and try one. Make sure they taste okay."

Marcus tried to keep a straight face because he knew what Roxy was doing, and he loved this side of her, a side he'd rarely seen. He watched Hunter pick one up, looking at it with narrowed eyes.

"It looks different." Hunter stared at it, then glanced at the bigger plate of deviled eggs. "The color is off."

"What the hell are you, a food critic?" Marcus rolled his eyes, really wanting Hunter to plop the chocolate deviled egg he was bitching about into his mouth. "Eat the damn thing already."

Hunter started to put it in his mouth, his eyes glancing at Roxy. "Ah hell no!" He pulled it away quickly. "This has chocolate in it."

Roxy chuckled. "It's not that bad."

"And you're lying." Hunter pointed the deviled egg at her. "You eat it."

"Chicken." Roxy dared him further, but Hunter was having none of it.

Emily laughed, her gaze on Hunter. "I can't believe you're afraid of a deviled egg."

"I'm not putting that nasty shit in my mouth." He shook his head. "Nothing against you or your cooking, Roxy, but there are things that don't belong together, and this is definitely one of them. Janna's little prego concoctions are nasty as hell."

"I'll eat the damn thing." Marcus grabbed it from Hunter and plopped it in his mouth, chewed and swallowed. "Not bad," he said with a nod.

Hunter watched him closely, then snorted. "Yeah, well whatever." Hunter grabbed one of the other deviled eggs and plopped it in his mouth. "You and Janna enjoy that nasty shit. I'll stick with the normal shit."

Hunter walked away with Emily giving Marcus the freedom to gag. "Goddamn, Roxy." He looked around, needing something to drink.

Roxy laughed. "I know, but Janna loves it."

Taking her hand, he pulled her toward a cooler. Reaching in, he grabbed a beer, opened it and filled his mouth, swished it around then spat it in the weeds before taking another drink, swallowing this time. "You could have warned me."

"Hey, don't blame me." Roxy grinned. "You took that and put it in your mouth so fast I didn't have time."

"Did you really try one?" Marcus pulled her closer to him, glaring down at her.

"No." Roxy shook her head. Her eyes were bright and filled with humor. "I lied."

"Prepare to be paid back for that," Marcus whispered with a wink.

# Chapter 3

Roxy had to calm her frantically beating heart as he held her. She wanted him to pull away, but she didn't. Her emotions were so confused that all she could do was stare up at him. Her hand was still in his, and she tightened her grip. In turn, he tightened his.

"Come on, guys." Leda hurried past them. "Grab some food."

Marcus finally stepped away from her and Roxy noticed Hunter trying to get Dell to eat one of her chocolate deviled eggs, who was looking at them suspiciously. Heading toward them, her breathing a little steady, she took the plate with a glare at Hunter. "Those are for Janna."

"What's in it?" Dell frowned down at the plate.

"Chocolate." Roxy laughed at the face Dell made, then took the plate to where Janna sat. "Here you go, Janna. Hunter's trying to give away your deviled eggs."

Janna picked one up and took a bite. "Oh my God, Roxy." She moaned, taking another bite. "These are freaking amazing."

"What is it?" Leda asked, looking at them. "I mean I know they're deviled eggs, but why are they dark like that?"

"Because they have chocolate in them." Janna took another one.

"Yuck!" Leda's face scrunched up in disgust.

"Just wait, Leda." Janna finished off another one. "When you're older and are having a baby, you're going to be eating all kinds of things that you never thought you'd eat. I've been having cravings like crazy. Poor Garrett doesn't know what to think."

Memories flooded Roxy's mind, her stomach knotting painfully. She'd had a similar craving in her past also, but that had ended abruptly.

"Hey, Roxy." Janna frowned up at her. "You okay?"

"Yeah, I'm fine." She nodded, needing to walk away for a minute. "I think I'll get myself a plate."

With everything going on and keeping her busy, her memories of the past had stayed buried just below the surface. But Janna's cravings had brought them back to the forefront, and she hated remembering. She sighed... like she could ever forget. Not really wanting anything to eat, she still picked up a paper plate and began filling it, staying away from the deviled eggs. She then headed toward the grill.

"Dog or burger?" Garrett smiled.

"A small hamburger, please," she replied, always feeling a little embarrassed with Garrett. She knew he probably thought she was or had been in love with him. But that was furthest from the truth. She may have had a hero worship thing going, but that was it. She appreciated what he did for her, what he was still doing for her, but nothing more. When she had made him dinner the night he showed up with Janna, it had made her feel terrible. Janna had been so sweet. Just thinking about it made her feel queasy with uncomfortable feelings.

"There you go." Garrett placed a small patty on her bun.

"Thanks," Roxy said, then stayed, her eyes plastered to her plate. She felt she should say something, but her mouth wouldn't work.

"You okay, Roxy?" Garrett asked, turning the hamburgers as he spoke.

God, she was a pathetic fool. "I'm really happy for you and Janna," she finally said before looking up at him. "I never, you know... it's just what you did for me...."

"You don't have to explain anything to me, Roxy." Garrett frowned down at her. She suspected he understood more about her than anyone else. He'd seen firsthand how she had been treated. He had saved her life. "And I do know, so never worry about that. Okay?"

Roxy nodded, never feeling so embarrassed in all her life, yet relief settled in her chest. She believed him. He may have at first thought she had some crazy infatuation with him, but not anymore. Walking away she felt somewhat better. She didn't want to always be on edge when around him and Janna. In truth, she and Janna had become good friends.

Seeing an empty table, she walked over and sat down. As she forced the food down, she looked around, realizing that Janna was her only real friend, other than Clare and Emily among the people in the town, but she was okay with that. She preferred it that way. She didn't trust easily, so it was the best situation for her. She was pulled from her thoughts when a certain voice stood out from the rest, and she looked that way.

Sadie Johnson stood talking with Linda and Deb, Emily's sister. Deb was another one she didn't care for. Even though she wanted to be alone, she was thankful when Clare spotted her and with a smile headed her way.

"Why are you sitting here all by yourself?" Clare plopped down next to her.

"What, you want me to go stand with Sadie and Deb?" Roxy snorted with a roll of her eyes.

"No, doesn't look like you have to. Here they come." Clare grimaced, making room for them.

Roxy moaned, but smiled when they came over and sat down at her table. Her eyes met Marcus who winked at her, but she blushed, looking away quickly.

"Can you believe Hunter's dating Emily?" Sadie snorted, then looked at Deb. "Sorry, don't mean to be rude, but she is so not his type."

"You don't have to apologize to me." Deb took a drink of whatever was in her red plastic cup. Rumor had it she liked her drinks strong. "I've thought the same thing. And I mean Garrett and Janna just don't make sense to me. She's so plain, and he's just… gorgeous."

Roxy rolled her eyes, catching Sadie's attention. "What? You think we're too harsh?"

*Keep it to yourself, Roxy,* she told herself. *Just keep your mouth shut.* Trying to listen to herself, she shrugged, pushing her picked-at plate of food away. "I just don't think it's any of our business who the Foster brothers chose for their mates or whatever they call it."

"So I guess you don't care who Marcus picks for his mate?" Deb chuckled, taking another long sip of her hidden drink.

"And why would I care, Deb?" Roxy turned her attention to Emily's sister, who she thought was a snobby bitch.

"Oh, I just heard some things about you and Marcus. That's all." Deb glanced at Sadie, and so did Roxy.

"Well, whatever you heard, you heard wrong, and if you have a need to know my fucking business, come and ask me." Roxy had enough of their shit. Her red hair only allowed her a certain amount of bullshit from stupid people, unfortunately.

"Oh, calm down." Sadie laughed, but the laughter didn't reach her eyes. No, her eyes were calculating and watching her closely. "You know how Deb is when she's drinking from her red cup."

Roxy didn't say anything to that, and neither did Deb, which clearly stated to everyone at the table who the ringleader was.

"She is right, though." Sadie's smile was fake with a hint of hatred toward anyone who may give her a run for her money. "Marcus does seem to spend a lot of time at the coffee shop."

"He's thirsty," Clare piped in with a sneer toward Sadie.

"Cute," Sadie snapped at Clare. "I think there's more to it than that, but if you're saying you and Marcus aren't, well, you know, then maybe I've been after the wrong brother."

Roxy laughed a real laugh. "Honey, maybe you're just the wrong woman."

"Ouch." Clare chuckled, then cleared her throat when Sadie glared her way.

Sadie stood, bringing her attention back to Roxy. "There's nothing wrong with me."

With that, she walked away and went straight to Marcus, who frowned when he saw her coming. Roxy didn't even flinch. She knew women like Sadie Johnson and if that was who Marcus wanted, then so be it, but she thought she knew him better than that.

"You really shouldn't piss her off," Linda said to Roxy. Linda looked more upset about Sadie flirting with Marcus than she felt. "She has ways of getting even with people."

Roxy watched the reaction Sadie was getting from Marcus and had to admit she was pleased. Sadie was beautiful on the outside, but a real bitch on the inside. Glancing from Marcus to Hunter then Garrett and even Dell, these men were more than handsome. It was normal for women to be attracted to them. She wasn't the jealous type really, never had been, and even more so after being married to a very jealous man. It was an ugly emotion.

"Linda, you're a nice person." Roxy looked her way. "Why do you even hang out with her?"

"She's okay. I mean she's not like that all the time." Linda frowned, glancing back at Sadie and Marcus.

"Didn't she and your ex Lance have a little something on the side?" Clare blurted, not looking at all sorry.

Roxy cocked her eyebrow at that, waiting for Linda to respond. Instead, Linda got up and walked away.

"Guess I should have kept that to myself." Clare smirked. "But the truth hurts."

"She did do that to Linda." Deb was still sitting there with a funny look on her face. "Yeah, I didn't agree with that at all. Linda was really hurt."

"Then why are you friends with her, Deb?" Roxy stood, grabbing her plate. "And the things she says about your own sister. If Emily was my sister and she said stuff like that, she'd be picking her teeth off the ground."

"She hasn't been too nice to Emily herself." Clare glared at Deb. "Isn't that right? You were the one who started the rumors about her and told everyone who would listen about Mable threatening Hunter to take her out. Hell, that's worse than what Sadie ever did."

Deb slammed her cup down, sloshing it all over and stood, the smell of alcohol filling the air. "Who in the hell do you think you are?"

"Well, I know what I'm not." Clare stood, going nose to nose with Deb. "Sadie's little bitch."

"Oh, okay." Roxy tossed her plate back down and got between the two women. "Let's calm down now, ladies. I don't think Janna would appreciate a throw down at her baby shower."

Roxy was a bit taller than the two women who were about to tear each other's hair out, and she had strength, managing to push them apart.

"I don't care what Janna would appreciate," Deb spat, then weaved before setting herself straighter. "She doesn't deserve Garrett, and she sure as hell doesn't deserve having his babies. As a matter of fact, I hope she…"

"Don't even go there," Roxy warned, her eyes narrowing, knowing exactly what Deb was getting ready to say.

"What?" Deb hiccupped, then sneered. "It would serve her right if she did lose—"

Roxy let go and punched her straight in the mouth, then headed for her as soon as her ass hit the ground. "I told you not to go there, you bitch." Roxy was on top of her, pounding her until strong arms grabbed her around the waist, pulling her off.

"Let me go!" Roxy fought against the tight grip that held her trapped and away from the bleeding bitch.

"Hey!" Marcus's voice was stern. "Calm down, killer."

"I'll kill her all right." Roxy slammed her foot down on his, making him release his hold, but Hunter was ready and stopped her from reaching Deb.

"You're psycho!" Deb screamed at her, wiping her nose, looking in horror at the blood.

"You don't even know," Roxy all but growled, pointing her finger at Deb. "If I ever hear you say anything like that again, you'll definitely see psycho."

"I didn't say anything." Deb sniffed, trying to look innocent, pissing Roxy off even more.

"The hell you didn't." Clare gave her a disgusted look. "And if Roxy hadn't gotten to you first, I would have. Shame on you."

Roxy started to calm down when she noticed everyone surrounded them. She pushed Marcus's hands off her. "I'm fine." She shrugged out of his hold. Her eyes went to Sadie, who grinned and shook her head at her.

"Well, I'm not fine." Clare clearly wasn't ready to let it go.

She knew that Clare was about to tell everyone what Deb had said, but her eyes met Emily's, who had just broken through the crowd to see what was going on.

"Don't, Clare." Roxy shook her head then nodded toward Emily. "Let it go."

Emily took one look around, her eyes narrowing on the red cup that was turned over with the contents spilled out on the table. She turned to Deb. "I think you need to leave."

"You're going to take their side over your own sister." Deb weaved again.

"Yeah." Emily frowned and sounded sad about that fact, but unmoved by Deb's fake, pitiful "feel sorry for me" voice. "I am."

"Fine." Deb looked around then seemed to realize she didn't have anything to take, so she turned to walk away, but put in a parting shot toward Roxy. "Don't think this is over."

"Okay, folks," Hunter said, grinning. "The women's throw down is over for now. I think it's time for presents. That was the preshow."

Roxy rolled her eyes but felt horrible when she glanced toward Janna who looked pale. God, she felt terrible. She should have let it go, but dammit, how could anyone let something so cruel like what Deb was insinuating go.

Falling into her chair, Roxy sighed, then looked at her hand. It hurt like a bitch.

"What in the hell was that about?" Marcus sat down between Roxy and Clare.

"Nothing." Roxy flexed her hand with a grimace.

Clare snorted. "If that bitch saying she hoped Janna lost her babies is nothing—"

"Clare," Roxy warned, but sighed again when Marcus slammed his hand on the table.

"She said what?" Marcus's voice was angrier than she'd ever heard.

"You heard me right," Clare said, ignoring Roxy. "And I swear when I see her again, I'm just going to punch her for the hell of it."

"She'd been drinking," Roxy said, knowing it was no excuse, but she was thinking of Emily, not her bitch of a sister. "I should have kept my cool. Sorry."

"If I would have known what had happened, I would have let it go longer." Marcus growled, his eyes narrowed dangerously.

"Yeah, well, I feel awful 'cause I totally ruined Janna's shower." Roxy did feel dreadful about that, but honestly, she would have done it the same damn way again.

"You didn't ruin anything." Marcus stood and pulled her with him. "Clare, run in and get Muhammad Ali here some ice for her hand."

"I'm fine," Roxy replied, even as her knuckles swelled. She'd had worse than this and survived. This was nothing.

Marcus and Clare ignored her, sitting her closer to where Janna was opening gifts. "Stay here, I'll be right back."

Roxy didn't argue, but she felt everyone eyeing her. She wanted nothing more than to go home. She had hoped to stay in the back while Janna opened all the baby presents, but there she was up front and center, eyes on her. And each sweet baby toy or clothing unwrapped was a stab to her heart.

Hearing a few people gasp, she turned to see Marcus walk from the house with a beautiful wooden bassinet. He placed it in front of Janna and Garrett, who stood by her side.

"This is from Roxy and me," he announced loudly and proudly. "I have the other one inside, but it looks like this one."

Tears stuck in her throat, behind her eyes, and anywhere else tears could stick, threatening to break through. Little pricks of pain exploded in her heart, then squeezed to the point of pain where she wanted to double over and crumple to the ground. Instead, she sat emotionless, staring at the bassinet, wishing once more that she had met Marcus Foster years ago. He would have stopped all the heartache she was afraid she'd feel for the rest of her life.

# Chapter 4

Marcus smiled at the excitement that Janna showed at his gift. He had always loved working with his hands and wood. His home was filled with things that he had made just waiting for his mate. At that thought, he turned to look at Roxy only to find her gone. His eyes searched and saw her rounding the corner of the house and disappearing. Leaning down, he kissed Janna's cheek, then took off after Roxy.

Tonight was the first time he had ever really seen any strong emotion from Roxy Patel. Even though it was anger, it was still an emotion. He could tell she was uncomfortable at losing control, but didn't think she should be. Deb was lucky he wasn't within hearing distance, not that he would ever hit a woman, but by damn, he sure would curse one, especially when something like that was said.

He also knew that Roxy didn't want to make a big deal out of it, not only for Janna's sake but for Emily. Deb was her sister and unfortunately, what Deb did or said could reflect badly on Emily. And honestly, he fell in love with Roxy even more than he already was at that moment.

"Roxy," he called out when he spotted her heading toward the coffee shop. When she didn't stop, he grew concerned. He knew she'd heard him. He caught up to her in the middle of the street and turned her toward him. "Where're you going?" Looking down into her face, he saw the tears reflected from the streetlight. Gently, he led her to the sidewalk, not knowing what was going on, what had upset her.

"Why're you crying?" He frowned, catching a tear with his thumb.

Roughly she swiped the tears away, sniffed and gave a bitter laugh. "Marcus, I can't do this." She sniffed again with another swipe. "I *really* can't do this."

Stepping back to give her space, he crossed his arms and stared down at her. "Do what?" He knew the answer but wanted to hear it come from her lips.

"Me, you, this." She couldn't meet his eyes; instead, she stared at his chest.

"Look me in the eyes and tell me that," he demanded, but kept his tone level.

Her eyes did shoot up toward him, but she quickly looked away. "What do you want from me?" she hissed, but she didn't sound angry. She sounded confused and lost. "Because honestly, whatever it is, I can't give it. I'm used up, done, and that's not fair to you. I have way too much baggage, more than you deserve to be saddled with."

"That was a mouthful," Marcus replied, his eyebrow cocked. "I think that's more than you've ever told me about yourself without actually telling me anything."

"Why?" Roxy asked, her face pale in the dim streetlight. "Why me?"

"Why not you?" Marcus shot back. He wasn't going to let her off that easy. He was done playing. He wanted her, he would have her, and it was time she realized that he didn't care about her baggage, her past, or anything else for that matter. What did matter was his intense need to help her heal, because that was the only way they could have a life together. Without her, he had no life. He knew it, his wolf knew it.

"I can't do this." This time anger fueled her words, and she turned to go into the coffee shop, but Marcus wasn't having it.

"Where's the woman who just beat the shit out of Deb?" Marcus turned her, searching her eyes. "I want to talk to her for a minute."

"What're you talking about?" Roxy tried to pull away from him, but it was a feeble attempt.

"That woman would answer my question and until she shows up and answers, we'll stand here all night." Marcus let her go, then leaned against the outside wall of the coffee shop, arms crossed and waited. He was a patient man. "Why not you?"

"Because I'm fucked up!" she shouted, then calmed immediately, visibly trying to gain control. "Is that what you wanted to hear?"

Marcus didn't want her to calm down. He wanted her true emotions. He wanted the real Roxy that she hid from others, from him. "I want to hear it all, Roxy." Marcus looked down at her and fought the urge to pull her into his arms like he wanted to. "But I want to hear it from the real Roxy, not the one you feel should interact with everyone. I want to hear it from the woman hiding inside you."

"I don't even know what that means." She lied, and he knew she lied. She knew exactly what he meant.

"Yes, you do." Marcus's gaze roamed the area to make sure they were still alone. He'd rather not have this discussion out in the open. "You know exactly what I mean and, Roxy, I'm not going anywhere. Until you look me in the eye and tell me you want nothing to do with me, I'm here. That there's no chance and mean it, I'm here and will be here. I'm a patient man. I've waited this long for my mate. I can wait longer."

Her eyes opened wide at the mention of mate. "Your mate?" She shook her head. "I can't be your mate. You're wrong. You have to be wrong."

Marcus chuckled. "I've been wrong plenty in my life, but not about this. You're my mate, Roxy Patel, *that* I know, and nothing short of my death will change that."

"Don't say that." Roxy frowned, wiping away a fresh tear.

"What, that you're my mate?"

"No, death. Your death," Roxy whispered, not looking directly at him.

"So, you do care." Marcus grinned, his wolf growing restless.

This time Roxy did look up into his eyes. "Of course I care, you ass."

"And there she is." Marcus chuckled, reaching out to touch her cheek. "The real Roxy Patel."

\*\*\*\*\*\*

Roxy stood there like an idiot, staring into Marcus's gorgeous brown eyes, mesmerized by everything about him. What she should be doing was running as far as she could, away from the heartbreak she knew would come. But instead, she just stood and then went into his arms as he pulled her to him.

"You're going to regret this," she whispered into his chest and was surprised when he responded because she was sure she had spoken those words to herself.

"Never." He held her tighter. "Whatever comes, whatever happens, know I'm beside you, Roxy. Since the day I saw you, I've been beside you."

God, she wanted to scream. Years she had wasted with the wrong man. Years had been spent with lies and pain beyond reason. Why now? Why was this happening? Was it a cruel joke being played on her and she would wake up in the nightmare that had been her life?

"I'm not divorced, Marcus." Roxy brought up one of the many things that haunted her. "I'm still married."

"And I told you I could remedy that." Marcus pulled her away, took her keys she had been holding in her hand, and opened the coffee shop door. "I will do exactly that. Now, let's fix us some coffee and talk."

Roxy walked in after he opened and held the door for her. Flipping on the lights, she quickly went to start some coffee. Her hands shook, her mind going a hundred miles a minute. She didn't know if she was ready to talk, but that wasn't really being fair to him. She waited for the coffee with her back turned to him, giving herself time to think. She would only answer his questions and offer nothing else.

She sensed him directly behind her, his woodsy scent filling her nose. Damn, he smelled good. The heat of his body warmed her. He reached above her, his body inches from hers as he took two coffee cups down with one hand and sat them next to her.

"Thank you," she said, licking her dry lips.

"You're welcome."

She sighed, whether in relief that he moved away or frustration, she didn't know. She was screwed, that much she did know. Just his proximity threw her for a loop, and with her growing feelings, she didn't know how she would ever be able to refuse anything he had to offer or ask of her.

When the coffee was done, she poured them both a cup and added sugar and cream. Suddenly she stopped and stared at the cups. She knew instinctively how much sugar and cream he liked in his coffee and never once had they even been on a date. Things were getting real, and she was getting scared.

Carefully, she picked up the cups, but he was there in a flash to take his from her. He put his free hand on her lower back and escorted her to a table, pulling out a chair for her until she was seated. Marcus then sat directly across from her.

"You sure can make one hell of a cup of coffee," Marcus said after taking a drink of the hot liquid.

"Plenty of practice lately," she responded automatically. She hated the waiting game and wanted to get this over with as quickly as possible. "What do you want to know, Marcus?"

He took another drink of coffee, staring at her over the rim. Setting the cup down, he leaned back in the chair. "Everything."

"That's not going to work." She shook her head, her index finger running along the rim of her coffee cup. "Ask me specific questions and I'll answer you."

"Fair enough." He nodded. "How bad was your marriage?"

Even though she expected tough questions, she was surprised at his bluntness. "Bad, but I'm sure there are worse marriages out there than what I had."

"I don't care about other marriages, Roxy." Marcus frowned. "I care about yours. If I don't know what you're running from, then I can't help you."

"It's not your job to fix me," Roxy countered, not at all comfortable.

"No, but it's my job to make sure you're happy, and I can't do that until I know you, and honestly, I don't know you as well as I need to know you." Marcus finished his coffee, then stopped her before she could stand to get him more. "Trust me."

She looked at his hand on her arm. It was a gentle touch, and she knew if she wanted to pull away, she could. The knowledge meant so much to her. "I met Bruce, my ex, five years ago on a blind date. He was nice, the perfect guy. We had similar tastes in a lot of stuff. We had dated for about six months before he asked me to marry him." Roxy shifted in her chair and finally pulled her arm out from under Marcus's hand. "It was a short engagement because he wanted to marry before he moved to Kentucky. He owns his own construction business."

"Construction?" Marcus frowned.

"None of the construction crews here are his," Roxy assured him. "Believe me, I paid close attention to that. But yes, there was more business in this area, so he was relocating his whole business. Had everything set up and ready to go. We married, moved away from my family and started our life."

Marcus was quiet, intently listening to every word. The only reaction he had was a cock of his eyebrow when she said he had moved her away from her family, and she knew what he was thinking. It was a classic move for an abuser, and he was right.

"We'd never lived together before and were both so busy with our separate lives. I was working and going to school to get my master's in business. All that changed when we moved here." She became silent for a minute.

"Where did you move from?" Marcus asked, seeming to want to pull her back to the present.

"California," she replied, her eyes becoming more focused.

"I guess moving from California to Lexington, Kentucky was a big adjustment?" Marcus smiled, cocking his eyebrow.

"It sure was, but I liked it. It just wasn't meant to be, though. The problems were gradual at first. He wanted me to set up the house before finding a job as well as hold off on school until the following semester. I agreed because it was pretty overwhelming." Roxy took another drink of her lukewarm coffee, then cleared her throat. "It wasn't until I had the house totally organized that I noticed every time I brought up going back to work and school, he would find something else for me to do involving the house. Nothing was right, though. He didn't like the paint color we chose and wanted it redone. He didn't like the way the kitchen cabinets were set up, so I had to rearrange them dozens of times until he was happy. He liked things organized. All forks, spoons, and knives had to be in a certain arrangement in the drawers, the cups, as well as plates, had their place."

She shifted again, her stomach tightening in knots, and a cold sweat broke out on her body. She was delving into something she wanted no part of, reliving her nightmare, something she swore she would never do. Glancing up, she saw understanding in Marcus's golden gaze as well as patience few had. He didn't say anything, just waited for her to continue, giving her time to collect her feelings and thoughts.

"He began getting angry if dinner was a few minutes late. It was unlike him. I would find out my mom would call, yet he never gave me the message to call her back. When I would call her, he would time my calls and stand over me, pressuring me to hang up. When we went to parties or out with his employees, I was given a briefing on what to wear as well as a list of things I was not able to bring up during conversation. Before we even left the house, I would have to parade in front of him until he approved of my appearance. The slaps started soon after I began questioning him on messages or talking back, pushing the issue of school. Once the slaps stopped controlling me, the real beatings started. It got to the point I couldn't leave the house until I healed. I was only hospitalized once when I tried to leave him, and he found me at the airport trying to get back to my family. I hated how weak I had become, but I had given up ever getting away from him." She swallowed hard, rubbing her forehead before dropping her hand to the table. "I really don't like talking about this."

"I really don't like hearing about it," Marcus responded, a tinge of anger in his voice. "But until this is out in the open, it's a burden between us, and we can't have that. I'm on your side, Roxy. Never doubt that."

Roxy nodded, then stood and grabbed herself another cup of coffee. She remained quiet until she sat back down. "I'm going to be up all night if I drink this." She chuckled quietly, shaking her head.

"I never sleep, so I'll keep you company." Marcus grinned with a wink.

Suddenly, she wanted Marcus to know everything. She wanted his support and his love, wanted his protection. She wanted him and everything that came with him. "He hurt me," she blurted, her hand squeezing against the coffee cup, splashing hot liquid onto her hand, but she ignored it.

Marcus didn't. "Careful." Standing, he went and grabbed a towel for her, wiping the liquid off her hand.

She took the towel away from him. "He had no right to hurt me." She used the towel to wipe off her stinging hand.

"No, he didn't," Marcus replied, a low growl following his statement.

She looked up at him, startled, experiencing something from a man for the first time: protectiveness. Her heart leaped at the sensation, the rightness of it.

# Chapter 5

Marcus seriously thought he was going to have to get up and leave, walk into the woods, and let his wolf loose for a minute just to get some fucking control. He had never wanted to kill anyone in his entire life, but this bastard was on his list and radar.

"Garrett never really told me what happened." Marcus had tried to get Garrett to tell him about the day he brought Roxy to town. He had never seen Garrett so pissed. He had only gotten a glimpse of Roxy that day, but her battered face and body were enough for him to know she had been badly abused. Garrett had called Clare in to take care of Roxy, and soon she was a part of the town. "He said that it was your story to tell."

Roxy actually smiled at that. "Garrett is a good man."

He pushed aside the twinge of jealousy. "He is."

"The last night I was with my ex we were eating dinner with an important potential client of his. I was tired and not really paying attention. The client's wife had asked me a question, and I asked her to repeat it with an apology." Roxy shivered, and Marcus wanted nothing more than to take her in his arms, but he knew it would be the wrong thing for him to do. He needed to let her finish. "We barely made it to the car before he started on me."

Marcus remembered that Garrett had been in Lexington during that time meeting with local pack leaders. He kept quiet, waiting patiently for her to continue. He wished he didn't have to ask her any of this but knew if they were to have a future, and it *was* time for their future to start, they could have no secrets between them. He had none to share; she already knew he was a wolf shifter, and that was the biggest secret he'd ever had.

"When he smacked me in the back of the head as I was getting into the car, it was the moment I'd had enough. Why that moment I don't know. I just knew that if he got me home, away from people, it would be bad. In public, he would only do things that people wouldn't see, like a pinch or a hard squeeze, warning me what was to come when we got home. The smack to the back of the head that night in a public parking lot was a warning that I may not survive this time. I was so scared but so damn angry, so I made sure to make a scene. I guess my actions pushed him over the edge. I remember getting out of the car screaming at him, hitting and slapping him, but that only lasted for a minute. Next thing I knew, I was slammed to the ground, and he was beating me in the parking lot of a nice restaurant in downtown Lexington." Roxy shook her head, a look of disgust on her face. "I barely remember Bruce being pulled off me. Memories of him being beaten by Garrett flashed through my mind, and then all I remember is waking up in a car. I begged him not to take me to the hospital, but to take me anywhere away from there. And that's when he brought me here."

He knew there was a little more to the story, but he didn't press. It was enough. "You've petitioned for a divorce?" He already knew the answer but needed transparency from there on out.

"Yes, but he hasn't signed the papers," Roxy responded.

"Have you had any contact since you've been here?" Marcus asked, thinking that she hadn't but wanted to make sure.

"No, he doesn't know where I am." Roxy frowned. "If he did, he would have been here by now. He doesn't like to lose or be made to look a fool."

"That's why you don't leave town?" Marcus refrained from saying her ex was more than a fool.

"Yes, there's no way I'm taking that chance." Roxy glanced away from him. "I'm fine here."

Marcus realized that there was no emotion coming from her. It was as if she were telling the story of someone else's life. He had plenty of emotions rolling through his body, but he was doing his best to control them so as not to scare her. If he'd been alone, he probably would have torn the hell out of the coffee shop.

"He's made you a prisoner," Marcus added, wanting to see if that would spark any emotion, but she just narrowed her eyes slightly.

"No, I'm finally free," she responded, then looked at him with a tilt of her head. "I'm really sorry about what happened at the shower. I should have had better control. I need to apologize to Janna."

"You've no reason to apologize. Anyone would have done the same." Marcus reached over and took her hand in his. The way his hand totally enveloped her smaller one made him feel more of a man, powerful and so protective he wanted to lean his head back and howl. "Thank you for telling me."

"Are you sure this is what you want?" Roxy's voice was doubtful, and he wanted more than anything to reassure her that she was exactly who he wanted. "That I'm the one you want."

"I've never been surer of anything in my life." Marcus let go of her hand to reach further over the small round table to cup her chin. "I knew the minute I saw you that you were mine. I actually wanted to kill my brother more than once because I thought you were in love with him."

She blushed and rolled her eyes. "I was never in love with Garrett. I just appreciated everything he did for me. He gave me my life back, gave me a place to live and work." She touched his hand on her chin. "I didn't know you had feelings for me."

Marcus laughed. "Like I said, I wanted to kill Garrett more than once over you, so yeah, there you go." His smile faded when she pulled away. He had a feeling he didn't know everything.

"There's one more thing you should know." Roxy stood, grabbed her coffee cup, and took it to the counter.

Okay, her walking away from him wasn't a good sign. He wasn't going to let her off that easily, so he stood and headed toward her. Stopping behind her, he turned her around. He lifted her face toward his, his knuckle under her chin. The emotion she had been missing was now blaring from her eyes as tears fell.

"I lost my baby that night in the filthy parking lot," she whispered as her face crumpled.

Not much shocked Marcus, but what she'd confided not only shocked him, but broke him. She grabbed on to him and clung tightly, releasing all the emotion he had wondered about. He wouldn't let her down. He would absorb all of it. Every single tear, anger, fury that she had he would take as his own. He felt dampness on his own cheeks and realized for the first time in his life, he cried.

\*\*\*\*\*\*

Roxy's whole body shook uncontrollably as she held on to Marcus, but the weight of what she'd revealed fell from her. No one knew. She hadn't told a soul about losing her baby that night. She had discovered she was pregnant a few weeks earlier and had planned to leave Bruce. No way was she going to bring a baby up in that kind of nightmare.

"I was so close." She cried into his chest. "So close."

He squeezed her tighter. "So close to what, Roxy?"

"Leaving him." She cried harder. "All I had to do was keep away from him, keep from making him angry, and I couldn't even do that. But I knew if I went home that night…. Either way, it didn't matter what I did… I still lost my baby."

"I'm so sorry." Marcus's hand pressed her head close to him, his fingers massaging her scalp. "I'm so damn sorry."

"Please don't say anything." Roxy knew he wouldn't, but felt better asking him. "No one knows."

"No one knows?" Marcus pulled away from her to look down into her face. "You didn't say anything? You went through that alone?"

Roxy nodded, trying to force her face back into his chest so he couldn't see her shame.

"Jesus." Marcus used his thumbs to wipe away some of her tears. "Why? Why didn't you say something?"

"Because I was ashamed of what I did," Roxy finally said, and it was the truth. She blamed herself. She knew without a single doubt that if Bruce laid hands on her, she would lose the baby; it had been her biggest fear. And yet, she'd pushed him knowing what the outcome would be.

"Listen to me." Marcus's voice became stern, losing its tenderness. "None of this is your fault. Do you understand me, Roxy?"

"But I knew and still baited him," Roxy spat, her anger growing when he didn't blame her. His reaction made no sense at all. "I shouldn't have—"

"Stop!" Marcus shook her gently. "Just stop. The blame lies with that son of a bitch. No man should hit a woman, ever. I promise you I will never lay hands on you. I would die before ever hurting you. Do you understand that?"

Roxy did know that. She wasn't afraid of Marcus Foster, never had been afraid of any of the Foster men because she knew they had honor. She'd seen them treat women with respect, so yes, she believed him with all her heart. "I know that, Marcus, and I'd never think that about you."

"Good," Marcus said, and she could see the tic in his jaw. He was angry, yet still she wasn't frightened as she knew it wasn't directed at her. "Have you seen a doctor since that happened, Roxy?"

"No." She shook her head. "I wasn't far along when it happened, maybe four weeks, if that." Tears once again clogged her throat and escaped in a cascade down her cheeks. It was long enough to care, to know she had something precious that she'd failed to protect.

"We're going to find you a doctor." Marcus held her as she stiffened. "I'm serious, Roxy. Do not argue with me on this. I'm stubborn, and when it comes to you and your welfare, stubborn doesn't even come close to what I will be."

She didn't know what to say. This was new to her. Instead of ordering her because of some control mindset, he was ordering her because he truly cared, and she felt it, believed it. Never did she believe she would be able to let a man close to her again, but Marcus, in his own way, had patiently worked his way into her life in small steps. It was actually the most they had ever really talked, even though they saw each other every day.

"Thank you," she finally said, then leaned up and kissed him on the cheek. He didn't try to push her for more. He accepted what she gave him and was fine with it; at least the smile on his face told her that.

"Never thank me for something like that, Roxy," Marcus replied, his eyes searching hers. "I'll always make sure you're taken care of."

"I know I have a lot of baggage, but I've been working on it. Tonight just set me off track." Roxy sighed with a frown.

"To hear someone say something like that is tough enough, but what you went through, it's totally understandable why you attacked the uncaring bitch." Marcus sneered. "Now come on, let's get you home so you can get some rest. I'll help you lock up."

Roxy nodded, then grabbed the dirty cups and headed toward the back. She flicked the lights on with her elbow and headed toward the sink. She put them down and started the water to wash them, but stopped. Her gaze went to the dirty knife still on the table, and then her eyes met Marcus's. He leaned inside the doorframe just watching her.

"You don't have to clean those tonight, Roxy," he said softly. "Actually, you can do whatever you damn well please. And that knife will be fine lying dirty right there on that table the rest of the night. As a matter of fact...."

Roxy watched as he pushed away from the doorframe and headed toward some drawers, opening them up, and she knew what he would find: the most organized drawer he had probably ever seen. Nothing out of place, each fork, knife, and spoon displayed to perfection.

"I think for a busy coffee shop, this is too organized." He glanced over his shoulder at her with a cocked eyebrow, giving her a choice to do something that she had considered so many times, but never felt right about. Now she did.

With a small smile, she walked over and edged her way between him and the drawer, her eyes never leaving his until she looked down into the drawer. With both hands, she grabbed the drawer and jerked, disrupting the contents. Her smile grew as she took back the power that had been taken from her for so many years. Grabbing a handful of knives in one hand and forks in the other, she mixed them up, dropping them, and then proudly closed the drawer.

"Felt good, didn't it?" He grinned down at her.

"Yes, it really did." She laughed then shook her head. "Dumb, huh?"

"Absolutely not." He touched her hair before running his fingers through it. "Anything else you want to fuck up while we're here?"

"I think that's enough for tonight." Roxy eyed the frosting knife again. "There's always tomorrow."

"Yes, ma'am, there is." He tenderly took her face and edged toward her, taking her focus off the dirty knife.

Roxy looked into his eyes and saw nothing but kindness reflecting in their depths.

"Can I kiss you?" He had lowered to the point their mouths were inches apart.

"You don't have to ask me, Marcus," she whispered, realizing that she wished with all her heart that he would kiss her.

"The first time, I do." Marcus leaned down, touching his mouth to hers softly.

She tilted her head and knew without a doubt she wanted more. She wasn't afraid of this man. The realization made her happier than she thought possible. Marcus had woven his way into her life. He hadn't erased her past, but he was making it more bearable. Disappointment flittered through her when he pulled away.

"Let's go." Marcus once again placed his hand on the small of her back and escorted her out, turning the lights off as they went. Once the door was locked, he took her hand and led her to the sidewalk.

"I don't want to be alone," Roxy blurted quietly in the darkness of the night.

"Good, because I wasn't going to leave you alone," Marcus promised as he wrapped his arm tightly around her.

# Chapter 6

Marcus walked toward Garrett's house with a huge smile even though he was quite pissed about leaving in the early morning hours from Roxy's small house. Once they got there, he knew she was uncomfortable, but as they started talking about things, she was at ease. They talked about everything from their childhood and growing up, and he'd loved every minute of it. They had laid on her couch, her with her head on his chest just talking until she fell asleep soon after. He'd savored the feeling of her in his arms as he also fell asleep until his phone went off.

His smile faded some at the reminder of what she had been through. They still had a long road ahead, but it was a start finally. He vowed to make sure she forgot her ex and what he put her through. She would never have a reason to fear again, not while he breathed.

Hurrying up the steps and through the front door, Marcus walked into the kitchen quietly. He knew Janna was probably still sleeping and didn't want to wake her. He made a beeline toward the scent of coffee.

"Well, someone looks chipper this morning." Hunter scrambled eggs at the stove but was staring at him.

"Shut up, Hunter," Marcus said, pouring him a cup of brew. "And when the hell did you start saying chipper?"

"What happened to you guys last night?" Hunter grabbed a plate, sliding his eggs on it. "One minute Roxy was beating the shit out of Deb, and the next she was gone and so were you."

"She felt bad about fighting with Deb," Marcus replied, not going into detail. "Where's Garrett?"

"Don't know." Hunter sat down at the counter and started eating. "What in the hell did she attack Deb for, not that it would surprise me. A lot of people want to beat up Deb."

"She made a comment about Janna and the babies." Marcus glanced around to see if Garrett had come in. "Roxy didn't want to say anything because of Emily."

"Good thing Emily didn't hear her." Hunter frowned, shoveling food in his mouth nonstop.

"Hear who?" Garrett walked in, his hair wet.

"Nothing," both Hunter and Marcus said at the same time.

"Jinx, bitch." Hunter pointed his fork at him.

"So what's up?" Marcus asked, ignoring Hunter.

"Jonah called me last night." Garrett looked at them both. "He's bringing in about ten shifters this morning who want to join our pack. He said he's certain about the majority of them, but we need to keep our guard up until we can truly trust them."

"Isn't that the way it always is?" Hunter asked with a frown.

"Yeah, we don't trust anyone until they prove their loyalty," Marcus confirmed. "Are they all male?"

"All but one," Garrett replied. "They should be here soon, so I want you both with me."

"No problem," Marcus replied, as did Hunter with his mouth full of food. "I'm going to run back to walk Roxy to the coffee shop, then I'll come back here. Did he give you any information on who he's bringing?"

"No, but I'm sure he checked them out as best he could." Garrett frowned. "I sent him to do a job and he did it. It's up to us to determine whether they're a fit for our pack. You know how dangerous that can be, so be on your toes."

"I was born on my toes," Hunter replied, shoveling food in his mouth.

"Do you ever stop fucking eating?" Garrett frowned at Hunter. "Jesus, you need to start chipping in on the damn food bill around here or eat at your own place. I know Emily cooks."

"I can't help it." Hunter finished his last bite then scraped his plate in the garbage. "I even ate before I got here and she cooks like a dream, but I like food."

"You're fat." Marcus eyed him. "Seriously, dude, you're getting a gut on you."

"Fuck you, man." Hunter lifted his shirt, showing not a six-pack, but an eight-pack. "This shit is solid."

"Yeah, solid fat." Marcus grinned and was ready for Hunter's punch, which he blocked.

"If you wake Janna, I will kick both your asses." Garrett growled, breaking them apart. "Now sit down and shut the hell up."

They both sat, and Hunter flexed his muscles.

"We need to make sure we keep an eye on our females, all of them." Garrett frowned. "I know I'll get challenged, but I'm not concerned with that. I'm concerned especially with Leda. She's coming of age…"

"Dude, she's already of age." Hunter's eyes narrowed. "And I will kill any son of a bitch who goes near her."

"Yeah, well, that's a good possibility of happening as we all know. Until they know our rules about the females, it could get ugly." Garrett was also frowning. "I've already talked to Dell—"

"Yeah, where is the big son of a bitch?" Hunter glanced at his watch. "Why isn't he here at the ass crack of dawn?"

"Is that eggs I smell?" Janna walked into the kitchen, rubbing her growing belly.

"What the hell is it with you and eggs?" Hunter rolled his eyes then stood. "No, don't even answer that. If that's all, bro, I'm out of here until later. I do not even want to start gagging this morning when she starts whipping out the chocolate syrup grossness."

"You are such a girl with all your whining and gagging." Janna yawned, leaning into Garrett.

"And you are such a fatty." Hunter winked at her.

"Babe, kick his ass for me," Janna said, but with a grin.

Marcus watched Janna and Garrett in a whole different light. He was happy for his brother to have finally found his mate and was determined that he and Roxy would be just as happy as Janna and Garrett were. He was suddenly anxious to get back to Roxy.

\*\*\*\*\*\*

Figuring Marcus got held up, Roxy locked up and stepped out into the brisk air. Compared to yesterday, it was much colder, the sky overcast. She was going to miss summer. This would be her first winter in Beattyville, and she was told the winter cold and snow could be brutal. Stepping out onto the dirt driveway, she took her time enjoying the walk. Her house was set just outside town off the main road, which she liked. Garrett, Marcus, and Hunter had all made sure her house was secure when they moved her in, and she had never once been afraid. The feeling of freedom trumped any fear she may have had.

Just as she got close to the end of her driveway, something caught her attention at the edge of the woods. Three wolves stepped out then stopped to stare at her. They didn't look familiar to her. She had seen all the wolves in town and knew without a doubt these were strangers. She didn't know if they were shifters or real wolves either; that was something she had been warned about.

A beautiful blonde girl stepped out of the woods behind them, her eyes narrowing on her before quickly looking at the wolves. Roxy wasn't sure, but she felt as if the girl was warning her. The biggest of the wolves shook before taking a step toward her.

"If you're looking for town, it's that way." Roxy pointed, her eyes never leaving the huge wolf. She didn't know what else to say and knew if she turned and ran back to her house, she would be way too slow.

"Let's go." The girl stepped in front of the wolf, blocking its path to Roxy. "You don't need to start trouble."

The wolf pushed her out of the way with its massive head, its eyes going back to Roxy. Her question had been answered—these were shifters, and she had a feeling she was in deep trouble. The wolf lowered its head, its golden eyes looking up at her before throwing its head back and letting loose with an ear-piercing howl.

The girl turned her head toward Roxy as if in slow motion. "Run!"

Roxy was rooted to the spot until her eyes met that of the girl. The urgency in her gaze had Roxy turning back toward her house, her feet moving and sliding in the wet dirt of her driveway. Taking a chance to look back, she saw the girl leap on the large wolf as it lunged toward her. The air burned her lungs as she ran; her house looked so far away. If she could just get inside, she had a gun and, by God, she would use it. Hearing pounding behind her, she knew she wasn't going to make it so instead, she veered off to the right and headed into the woods.

This was mountain region, so nothing was flat. She grabbed bushes and trees as she continued down the steep incline, turning her head to see how close to being caught she was. The girl was still fighting against the wolf, the other two must have stayed behind, or they were circling in front of her. The thought of that chilled her to the bone. Just when she thought she had found happiness, she was going to die.

Anger overtook her emotions, her eyes scanning everywhere as she ran. Branches snapped against her face as she raced through thick brush. Seeing a tree, she knew what she needed to do. Running faster than she ever had in her life, she reached the tree and took a leap, thankfully grabbing the long branch. Quickly, she pulled herself up and began to climb, her breath coming in sharp gasps. Not being able to get much further, she stopped and looked down. The wolf was now below her, clawing at the tree, its loud, aggressive growls echoing in the woods. She reached out and broke off a large branch, almost toppling herself out of the tree, and then threw it at the wolf, hitting him on its large nose.

"Get the hell away from me!" she hissed, then looked up the hill to see the girl tripping her way toward them, bleeding badly from her face and holding her side.

"You will not ruin this for me, Carl!" Even hurt, the girl's voice was strong and full of fury. "Damn you!"

Seeing the girl fall and the wolf stalk her way, Roxy knew she needed to do something. She couldn't let the woman be harmed for trying to help her. Looking around, she wondered how far away she was from town. Had she run toward it or away? She didn't know. She remembered Marcus telling her a while ago, that if she had any trouble to scream as loud as she could, and they would hear her.

Knowing she had to do something and fast, she opened her mouth and screamed louder than she had ever screamed in her life. Fear, fury, and pure determination escaped from her mouth. She'd be damned if she became a victim again or watched another woman become a victim of some piece of shit.

# Chapter 7

Marcus headed out of Garrett's to go get Roxy and walk her to work. Before he took three steps after clearing the porch, he heard a wolf's howl. He became alert, his eyes going directly to where Dell was quickly dragging himself from under a car he was working on. Their eyes met.

"That's not one of us," Dell said as he jumped up.

Taking off in a run, Marcus headed straight toward the direction the howl came from and Roxy's. Hunter and Garrett quickly caught up. As they left the main road, Hunter and Garrett continued straight to make sure they had the direction correct. Rounding the corner, Marcus noticed two wolves standing at the edge of the woods looking across the driveway toward the trees, but Marcus passed them heading toward Roxy's house.

Stopping at her door, he pounded, yelling her name. Nothing. She wasn't there. Anger and fear enveloped him as he turned toward the two wolves to see Dell, Garrett, and Hunter surrounding them with others in their pack running toward them.

Rage propelled him toward the two wolves. He knew Roxy wasn't at the coffee shop because the lights were off when he'd passed. Somebody better be answering questions and real quick. Before he reached them, a scream split the air sending birds flying out of the woods. Without breaking stride, Marcus cursed and shifted in a flat-out run.

As soon as he hit the woods, he picked up her scent. He also picked up the smell of blood and he swore if she had shed one drop, someone was going to die. Even as quick as he was going, he noticed the damage to the brush and knew this was the path Roxy had taken. He heard her voice, strong and angry, shouting. His relief was swift that she sounded fine. Breaking through the thick brush, the first thing he saw was a blonde woman lying still on the ground. His eyes rose to the wolf who was walking away from her toward a tree. Glancing up, Marcus saw Roxy throwing branches down at the large wolf, screaming at it to shoo. She was actually cursing and shooing a full-grown wolf.

He knew the wolf was too preoccupied with his prey to realize the danger, so Marcus took advantage and blindsided the bastard. They rolled away from the tree and Roxy, which was what he wanted. The other wolf was strong, but Marcus was stronger. He refused to lose to the son of a bitch who had been intent on harming his mate. Taking a quick glance to make sure Roxy was still safe was a mistake. Sharp teeth bit into his shoulder making him howl in rage.

He had no idea how long the fight continued, but he did know he had definitely been in a fight. He would have to be in wolf form to heal from this. The bastard finally started to bend to his will until finally, the wolf sat in front of Marcus with his head down in submission. Marcus paced in front of the son of a bitch, growling and nipping.

"That's enough," Garrett ordered, anger shaking his voice.

Marcus gave one more growl before he shifted back. The pain ripped through his shoulder, pissing him off even more, but he gave the wolf who remained in form one last look before turning back to Roxy who had stayed in the tree with Hunter on guard at the base.

"You're hurt!" she cried out and started to climb down.

"Stop!" Marcus ordered her, not wanting her to attempt the climb down just in case she fell. He turned toward Hunter. "Get me some clothes, at least sweatpants."

"Already on it." Hunter frowned, glancing at his shoulder. "Leda is coming with them. And you need to shift back. That shoulder looks bad, bro."

"What?" Roxy said from the tree. "What looks bad? Marcus, are you okay?"

"I'm fine." He shot Hunter a warning look.

"You're naked," she blurted with a blush.

"And that's why you're still in the tree." Marcus chuckled. "Just stay put until I can come up and get you. Are you hurt?" He was impressed she had climbed the tree, and relieved by her quick thinking.

"Oh, for shit's sake." Roxy shook her head. "I got up here, I can get down. You're hurt and shouldn't be climbing up after me."

"Dammit, Roxy." Marcus glared up at her, ready to catch her if she fell as she made her way down the tree.

"Here." Leda ran up, keeping her eyes averted as she tossed the sweats in his direction.

He took his eyes off Roxy for a second to catch the sweats and put them on, before returning his gaze to Roxy and her ass. Jesus, he was getting hard watching her shimmy down the fucking tree. It was always the same. After they had shifted and fought, sex was the main outlet for their energy. Once she was close enough, he reached up and grabbed her, lowering her to the ground. Turning her toward him, he checked her over.

"Are you hurt?" He frowned at the scratch on her face. "I'm going to kill that son of a bitch."

"No, you aren't." Grabbing his arm, she stopped him. "I'm fine."

Marcus did his best to control himself, but seeing her hurt, even if it was just scratches, sent his rage past the point of control. "Did he touch you?" he asked with a low growl, his eyes searching hers for the truth.

She reached up and touched his cheek, bringing his focus back to her. "Marcus, I'm fine."

"Were you shooing a wolf?" Marcus glared down at her.

"Yes, but unsuccessfully." Roxy looked embarrassed, but a nervous laugh escaped her lips. "I didn't know what else to do."

"Just an FYI, shooing doesn't usually work on a full-grown wolf, Roxy." He pulled her to him and held her tight. Thank God she was fine, because he didn't know what he would do if something happened to her.

\*\*\*\*\*\*

Knowing she was safe, the effects of being scared to death made her tremble, or maybe it was seeing Marcus completely naked standing under the tree staring up at her. One thing for sure was he was all man. Hearing a woman's voice, Roxy pulled away and looked toward the blonde woman Dell was helping to her feet.

"Who are they?" she asked Marcus, not leaving his embrace.

"Not sure, but my guess is the shifters that Jonah was bringing in." Marcus frowned, also looking toward the woman. "Are you sure you're okay?"

"Yes, I'm okay," Roxy replied, her tremors lessening in his arms. Glancing up the hill she had come down, she frowned. How she managed down that hill and up the tree without being caught shocked her. Her gaze went toward the blonde woman who Dell was talking to.

"Sit here for a minute." Marcus led her to a broken log and eased her down. "I'll be right back."

She nodded, still looking at the woman who seemed hurt. Soon the wooded area they were in filled with people, most she knew, some she didn't. Marcus stood with Garrett and Hunter talking to the wolf who had tried to attack. Marcus lunged at the naked man, who had shifted, but Garrett stopped him. She couldn't hear what was being said, but Marcus was angry, fighting against Garrett's hold.

Filled with a nervous energy that left her bobbing her knee up and down, she couldn't sit any longer. Standing, she quickly realized her legs were weak and shaky. She ambled toward the blonde woman, who like her, sat alone. Dell had left to talk to Jonah who had also shown up.

"Thank you," Roxy said, standing over the woman.

The woman glanced up at her, fresh blood seeping from the long gash along her forehead. "You're welcome," she replied, swiping the blood to keep it from going in her eyes. "I'm really sorry."

"You've nothing to be sorry for." Roxy frowned, searching for something to give the woman to stop the blood from running. Of course being in the woods, there was nothing. Spotting a pointed rock, she bent and picked it up, then stabbed a hole through her thin shirt under her jacket. After ripping a strip, she knelt down, moved the woman's blonde, blood-soaked hair out of the way and gently held the cloth to the angry-looking wound. She noticed the woman clutched her ribs, her breathing coming in short gasps. "How badly are you hurt?"

"I'll be fine." She smiled, then grimaced when the smile caused her pain.

"What's your name?" Roxy felt the dampness of the dirt but ignored it.

"Roslyn, but I go by Ross." She took the cloth from Roxy's hand and peered at it.

"Tomboy, huh?" Roxy grinned, hoping to take the woman's mind off all the blood that had soaked the cloth. "I'm Roxanna, but I go by Roxy. If it wasn't for you, I never would have been able to escape, so again, thank you."

"Didn't I tell you to stay over there?" Marcus walked up, standing directly over her.

"Yes, you did," Roxy replied, glaring up at him. "But I wasn't going to sit there and watch her bleed to death. If it wasn't for her, I wouldn't have been able to get away."

"Is that true?" Marcus glanced at the woman, his eyes narrowing.

"Carl is trouble." The woman glared over at where the man named Carl was now standing with a pair of sweats someone had given him. "You don't want him in your pack, mister."

Roxy watched Marcus closely to see how he was going to respond. He had turned to look at the man, anger clouding his eyes.

"I'm Marcus." He turned back to the woman. "And don't worry, he won't be."

"She's hurt." Roxy stood, dusting the mud off her knees. "She needs a doctor."

"No, I don't." Ross shook her head and stood slowly, a moan escaping. "I just need somewhere safe to shift, and I'll be fine."

"You can stay with me," Roxy offered, but Marcus stopped that real quick.

"Ah, no, she can't." Marcus's tone clearly indicated that was final. "We'll find you a safe place."

"She'll be fine at my place." Roxy put her hand on her hip, glaring at Marcus. "It's the least I can do."

"Excuse us," Marcus said, pulling Roxy toward the hill, then stopped. "She will not be staying with you. We don't know who she is, who any of them are and until then, they'll be watched closely."

"Well, that makes no sense at all." Roxy frowned, looking back at the woman. "She tried to help me, not hurt me."

"I'm not budging on this, Roxy." Marcus rolled his shoulder with a hiss of pain. "But I do promise you she will be well taken care of."

Knowing he was hurting, Roxy caved. "Okay, I just feel bad that she was hurt and you were hurt because of me."

"This wasn't because of you, Roxy," Marcus assured her. "And by the way, how in the hell did you end up in that tree?"

"I was going into work when three wolves came out of the woods at the end of my driveway. I wasn't sure if they were shifters or real wolves, but I knew I'd never seen them before. The woman came out and took one look at me. I knew then I was in trouble. The one started stalking toward me and then howled. Before he could take off after me, Ross—"

"Ross?" Marcus's brow dipped into a frown.

"Yeah, her name is Roslyn, but she goes by Ross. She jumped on him and screamed for me to run." Roxy glanced at his shoulder before looking back into his eyes. "I tried to make it to the house, but I knew I wouldn't be able to unlock the door in time so I headed toward the woods. She fought him all the way down the hill, and if it wasn't for her, he would have caught me. I saw the tree and knew if I made it up there, he couldn't get to me unless he shifted."

"You're a very smart woman." Marcus cupped her cheek, running his thumb close to the stinging scratch on her face.

Roxy glanced up the hill, then to the tree. "No, I'm a very lucky woman."

"Come on, let's get you home. I have to take care of some things, and then I need to heal." Marcus clasped her hand and led her toward the base of the hill.

"I have to open the coffee shop. I'm already late." Roxy tried her best to get up the hill on her own because she knew his shoulder was hurting, but it was nearly impossible for her. Midway up, he stopped and picked her up after she slipped for the hundredth time. "No, your shoulder."

"Is fine," Marcus said against her hair. "We're almost there."

She figured he would let her down as soon as they broke through the woods at the top of the hill, but he didn't. It looked like the whole town had shown up. Everyone stood around, and all eyes landed on her and Marcus.

"You can put me down now," Roxy whispered, but couldn't help the rush of pleasure from being held by him. He looked damn good without a shirt on and even with it being cold, his body heat warmed her better than an electric blanket.

"Nah, it's time this town knows exactly who you belong to." Marcus grinned down at her. Then in front of everyone, he kissed her soundly on the lips.

She actually groaned when he pulled his lips from hers. A large masculine grin spread across his face, making her blush. She looked away only to see Sadie Johnson glaring at her. Maybe he was right. It was time this town knew that she and Marcus belonged to each other.

# Chapter 8

Marcus left the coffee shop reluctantly, but he knew he was close enough to keep an eye on the building and didn't plan on being gone long. Roxy had assured him she was fine, but still, walking out that door had been the hardest fucking thing he'd ever done. But he had work to do and his alpha demanded him to be present.

They had taken all the new wolves to Jonah's, and that was where Marcus was headed. His shoulder hurt like a bitch, and he knew if he didn't shift soon, he might have permanent damage, not to mention an infection setting in.

Walking inside Jonah's, he heard his alpha talking and respectfully found himself a spot in the back of the small room. The wolf who'd been after Roxy stood in the middle of the room with the other two wolves slightly behind him. Marcus took pleasure in the fact he looked like he was in as much pain as he was.

"You came into my town, attacked someone under my protection, and expect me to keep you on as part of my pack?"

"I wouldn't have hurt her," Carl said, not realizing Marcus had walked into the room.

"Bullshit," a female voice spoke out.

"Shut up, Ross," Carl growled her way.

Dell smacked the guy upside the head. "You shut the fuck up, asshole."

Marcus stepped forward. "I agree with her." He nodded toward Ross. "Bullshit. You chased a human female through the woods, down a small mountain and scared her enough to send her up a tree to escape you. Not to mention she is my mate. You're lucky you're breathing right now, motherfucker."

"I didn't know she was mated." Carl glared at Marcus. "She's not marked."

"It doesn't fucking matter." Marcus headed toward him, but Hunter stepped in front of him, stopping his progress.

"Chill, brother," Hunter warned him. "Remember who you are."

"She is a female. We treat our females with nothing but respect," Marcus shouted around Hunter, then looked at Garrett. "He does not belong here, and I can pretty much guarantee you if he does stay, he'll die at my hand."

Garrett gave Marcus a nod but didn't say a word.

"And as for you." Marcus turned his focus on the other two men standing behind Carl. "You let a female defend my mate while you did nothing?"

"He's our alpha," one of them said, which made Carl puff out his chest.

"There's only one alpha in this town, and that fucker is not him." Marcus shook his head and turned toward Garrett. "I vote for these three to go. I've already stated my reason why on that asshole, and these two... I don't think I need to say anything. He said it all in announcing who he thinks is the alpha here."

"That's my vote also," Hunter added, Dell nodded, and Jonah also gave his nod.

"They were given the rules before we were even on our way here." Jonah's hard stare was directed toward Carl. "They all agreed, even those three."

"How are you involved with them." Marcus turned to look at the woman who had helped Roxy.

"He's my stepbrother." Ross pointed to Carl. "And voting him out would be in everyone's best interest."

"You bitch!" Carl spat her way and took a step toward her.

"Make one more move, and it will be your last." Dell's deadly tone filled the room, stopping him instantly.

"I should have killed you when I had the chance." Carl growled at her with a snap of his teeth.

"Yes, you should have," she shot back.

Carl turned toward Garrett. "I challenge you for this pack."

"Please accept," Hunter snarled toward Garrett, but his eyes never left Carl.

"It would not be a challenge since you're injured," Garrett responded, his tone full of disgust. "And because you disrespected one of my high-ranking member's mate, he has the right to accept the challenge in my place, and we all know how that will turn out."

"It's a shame to see an alpha afraid to accept a challenge," Carl baited, but Garrett just smiled as he took a step toward him.

Grabbing Carl around the throat, Garrett lifted him off the ground with one hand. "You just made my decision simple." The man's feet began to twitch as Garrett lifted him higher. "You are banished from this pack. If you return, it is a definite death sentence without trial. I will warn other packs in the area about you and your disrespectful practices."

Garrett tossed him toward the other two men.

"I'll see that they leave the area," Dell volunteered quickly.

"Do not take my mercy as weakness," Garrett warned all three of them. "If I see you back, even hear about you in this area, you'll be hunted down and will not be given this mercy twice."

Dell grabbed Carl by the back of the neck, pushing him toward the door. Carl stopped and glared toward Ross. "You coming?"

"No." She shook her head. "Even if I'm refused here because of you, I'll find my own way."

"Stupid bitch," Carl sneered, still rubbing his neck where Garrett's handprint was displayed. Then he looked at Marcus.

"If you want to leave here alive, I suggest you keep moving with your fucking mouth shut," Marcus warned with a cocked eyebrow, daring him to utter one word. Once Dell, along with a few others, ushered Carl and the other two out the door, he relaxed, but only slightly. There were still strangers among them and after this, he was rethinking making their pack stronger by bringing others in.

"I was never loyal to him. He was not my alpha." The woman looked from Marcus to Garrett. "If you want me to leave, I will."

Garrett looked away from her without answering to the other six, his eyes meeting each one. "Have no doubt that we are a strong pack. I am a strong and just alpha, as you have seen. What Carl did warranted death, but I have shown mercy and will say again, do not mistake my mercy for weakness, because you will greatly regret it." Garrett's voice boomed through the small room. "For those of you who want to stay, you will follow my rules. You will respect not only my pack but the humans who reside in this town. Is that understood?"

The remaining shifters nodded, their eyes wide.

"I have a different set of rules here. Women are not for your taking. We do everything here the shifter way other than that of mating. The woman has to be in full agreement. We do not force our will on the women as has been the way of many packs. I am alpha, and you will abide by my rules. You will be loyal to not only me but everyone in this town, shifter and human alike." Garrett again looked at each one in the eyes. "Know that anything my brothers, Marcus and Hunter, say to you is coming from me. Is that understood?"

Most nodded in agreement, a few agreed verbally.

"Each one of you will be interviewed by one of us, but until then, you will stay with Jonah under his charge by my word." Garrett turned to look at Ross. "You have already displayed your loyalty by saving one of ours and putting your life in danger. You will have a place to stay by the end of the day."

"Thank you." The woman bowed her head to Garrett in respect.

"For now, Jonah will find you a room here so you can shift and begin to heal." Garrett gave Jonah a nod. Jonah waved her over and walked out of the room with her. Garrett waited for her to leave before continuing, "It's going to be a long day so get comfortable." Garrett dismissed them.

Marcus had relaxed and was leaning against the wall. His eyes watched each new individual closely, but it was hard to focus. His shoulder was killing him.

"You need to shift and heal." Garrett looked at his shoulder and frowned. "Infection is already setting in."

Marcus knew what Garrett said was true. A wolf's bite was vicious, and if not taken care of properly, it would, in fact, turn bad very quickly. "I'll help you interview, then I'll shift."

"No, you will do it now," Garrett ordered. "You're no good to me dead."

"Go shift, man." Hunter nodded to him. "We got this, and Dell will be back soon. With four of us interviewing, it will go quickly."

"Shit," Marcus grumbled, hating being hurt. He was a bad patient when he was sick or injured. "Should've killed the bastard."

"Probably," Hunter replied, both teasingly and serious. "I hope that wasn't a mistake."

Marcus agreed as he walked out Jonah's front door. Automatically, his gaze traveled to the coffee shop. He headed that way, needing to make sure she was okay one more time before he found a place to shift and heal.

******

Roxy was glad it had been busy. With all the activity, the coffee shop had been packed, especially since she and Clare hadn't had time to take coffee to the construction workers. So instead, they came into the shop. She finally had a slow period so she was able to straighten up in back while Clare manned the front.

She was worried about Marcus. His shoulder looked bad and she knew it hurt. Glancing once again at the frosting knife on the table, she smiled when her stomach didn't dip with nausea. Walking over to it, she picked it up and stared at the dried frosting. Glancing at the drawer, she crossed the floor and opened it to see the silverware still in the messy state she and Marcus had left it in last night. With her free hand, she messed them up a little bit more and then closed the drawer, her smile growing. When she turned to the sink, her eyes met Marcus's, who leaned in the doorway still shirtless.

"You are beautiful." His voice was low as his eyes searched her face. "You need to smile like that more often."

Heat filled her cheeks, and she knew she blushed, but she also noticed how pale he looked, his eyes glassy. Tossing the knife into the sink, she rushed toward him. His shoulder looked worse. "You need to see a doctor." She touched his cheek and frowned. "You've got a fever."

"I need to shift," he replied, pressing his cheek into her hand. "I'll be fine."

"What are you waiting for, Marcus?" She didn't like how pale he looked. She suddenly realized she couldn't lose him. "Shift."

He reached up, taking her hand in his, then kissed her palm. "I wanted to check on you first. Are you sure you're okay?"

"I'm fine. Now please go shift," Roxy urged. "I don't know what I'll do if something happens to you."

A grinned tipped his lips. "So you do care for me?"

"Of course I care for you." She rolled her eyes. "Now please, go take care of yourself."

"I'd walk through hell for you, Roxy. Don't you know that?" Marcus pushed away from the doorway and nudged her body further into the back with his. He bent his head and kissed her, and not with the sweet soft kisses he had been giving her. This time it was a hard promise that she was his. He pulled her against him with his good arm, deepening the kiss.

Roxy was sure she was going to pass out from lack of air, but she didn't want him to stop. She would happily faint if he just kept going, but he pulled away, and she wanted to cry. Never had she been kissed like that.

"Wow," Roxy whispered, her wide eyes staring up at his hooded gaze.

"Yeah, wow." His deep voice vibrated through her. He then shifted his body and grimaced. "Okay, I need to go. Hunter and Dell are going to keep an eye on you until I can get back. Don't leave until one of them comes and walks you home."

"Where are you going to go?" Roxy didn't like the idea of him being alone.

"I've got a small place outside town. I'll head there," Marcus replied. He leaned down and pressed his lips to hers again. This time it was a short peck.

"Alone?" She frowned. "No, I don't think so."

She grabbed his hand and stepped into the front of the shop. Clare stood behind the counter staring out the window. "Hey, what else you need me to do?" Clare asked, seeing them come from the back.

"You think you can close up for me?" Roxy asked, hoping Clare wouldn't mind.

"Yeah, of course." She glanced at Marcus's shoulder and cringed. "You need to get that shoulder taken care of."

"That's what we're going to do." Roxy led Marcus toward the door. "Just leave the dishes in the back. I'll do them tomorrow morning. Thanks, Clare."

"No problem," Clare called out. "Let me know if you need anything else."

"Good girl." Marcus squeezed her hand as they headed toward the sidewalk.

"What?" Roxy squeezed back as she looked up at him, not liking his color at all.

"Leaving dirty dishes and shit." He chuckled. "I'll make you a rebel yet."

Roxy smiled, knowing without a doubt she loved this man. No matter what her past had thrown at her, it didn't make her unlovable, and it didn't stop her from having strong emotions. She loved Marcus Foster and right now the most important thing was to get him well.

The closer they got to her house, she noticed his stride, which was usually long and with purpose, had slowed. He also stumbled once, terrifying her. "Marcus, please shift." She grabbed his elbow to steady him, and he leaned into her.

"I'll wait until we get to your house." His eyes looked up from the road to search where they were. He seemed still aware of what was going on and alert, but he was fading fast.

"Is there anything I can put on your shoulder?" She frowned, realizing she didn't know what in the hell she was doing. She had taken care of her own wounds so figured it would be the same, but he was a wolf. Was it different for them? She didn't know.

"After I shift, if you have any peroxide or alcohol, you can apply that." Marcus stumbled again. They were in her driveway and stopped in front of her house.

"Anything else I should know?" She looked up at him, even ready to catch him if he collapsed, not that she could support his weight, but she'd damn well try.

"Don't be afraid of me." Marcus stared down at her, touching her face gently. "Please don't be afraid of me. My wolf would never hurt you. I will heal ten times faster in wolf form."

"I'm not afraid, Marcus." Roxy rose on her tiptoes and kissed his cheek. "Now shift so you can get better. I need you."

Pulling her to him, he kissed her hard. "Love you," he whispered against her lips as he pushed her back carefully. She never knew exactly how she would react to hearing those words again from a man, but hearing them from Marcus, she believed him. She wasn't afraid of them, nor him. She trusted again when she had thought trust would be something she could never do again with a man.

His body shook almost violently, and Roxy cringed knowing it had to be hurting his shoulder. Within seconds, a large wolf stood before her, his eyes staring up at her, then away as if uncomfortable. The wolf before her was Marcus and she knew it. Taking a step closer, she reached out, putting her hand in its beautiful, soft gray and white fur.

"And I love you," she said to the wolf. "And I'm not afraid."

She walked slowly to her door, the wolf limping beside her. She unlocked the door, and before she could walk in, he used his massive head to nudge past her and blocked her entrance while looking around her small home. Roxy sighed, realizing even in wolf form Marcus was making sure she was safe. Her love deepened to the point it was painful, but the sensation made her smile.

She went to the kitchen to search for her peroxide, got a bowl of warm water, and then walked out to see Marcus lying on the hard floor. She went to her bathroom and collected a clean towel, then returned to Marcus.

"Marcus," she whispered, hating to wake him, but no way was he staying on her floor. His eyes opened, looking surprisingly alert. Lifting his head slightly, he glanced around until he settled back on her. "I'm sorry, but you need to get off that hard floor. Come on."

She headed toward her bedroom and opened the door, but Marcus remained on the floor staring at her.

"Come on," she urged and stopped herself from snapping her fingers. Something she did when she wanted her little childhood dog to follow her. "Don't try me, Marcus Foster. You are not lying on my floor, and don't think I won't try to pick you up."

She could have sworn he smiled, but it was hard to tell. With slow movements, he stood and limped toward her. She led him into her bedroom. He paused, taking in the surroundings. She took that time to pull the covers down to the end of the bed and then stepped aside so he could climb up onto the mattress. He hesitated, but then limped her way and jumped up, then lay down.

Roxy climbed up on the bed before dipping the towel in the water she'd set on her nightstand. With great care, she cleaned the wound. She hated every moment, knowing it hurt, but Marcus didn't flinch or whimper in pain. Feverish eyes watched her and the more she stared into them, the more she saw Marcus. How odd this was, yet it felt so right. This man could be the famous bigfoot, and it wouldn't faze her. She loved him.

Soon after, she had the wound clean and the dreaded peroxide applied, which seemed to hurt her more than it hurt him. She'd been the one hissing as she'd applied it, watching it bubble and work on the angry-looking wound.

Once finished, she sat everything on her nightstand and watched him. He had finally closed his eyes. Able to relax knowing he was resting and healing, she gave herself a moment to consider all that had happened and just how she felt. Her attraction to Marcus was off the charts, which surprised her somewhat. Seeing him naked earlier had sent a spark through her body, making her realize she missed making love. Bruce, being the bastard he was, had always made sure she was taken care of in bed. Possibly it was a pride thing for him to make sure she was satisfied. She wasn't afraid of sex, she actually really missed it. Not with Bruce, of course, just the act. Rolling her eyes at her thoughts, she sighed. She must really be hard up if staring at a wolf was getting her all worked up. What the hell was wrong with her? An image of him standing naked below the tree flashed through her mind. He was a damn fine male specimen. She grinned at that thought, then yawned.

Taking care not to hurt Marcus, she stretched out beside him, her hand buried in his fur. Before long she fell asleep.

# Chapter 9

Marcus woke feeling better, not a hundred percent, but much better. He was still in wolf form as he lay, his eyes finding Roxy curled up next to him. She had taken such good care of him during his time of healing. She had cleaned his wound, made him drink, and gave him love. No one could ask for anything more than that. He knew Hunter had been there plenty, checking on him as well as her, and he owed his brother for that. Garrett had also stopped in to check on everything. He stood, careful not to wake her. He needed to shift and shower. He also needed to piss. He hated pissing in wolf form. He backed off the bed and stood still, making sure she remained asleep. He knew she had to be exhausted.

Taking a step, he winced when his claws clipped on the hardwood floor loudly. Glancing at her, Marcus watched her stir, but she remained asleep. He then shifted. He worked his shoulder back and forth, trying to see if the damage was repaired. It appeared better but felt a little weak. He knew that was normal. He also knew without looking down he had a massive hard-on. Worried she would wake up to him staring down at her with his cock hard and ready, he quietly walked out of the room.

He desired nothing more than to crawl into bed and bury himself deep inside her, but that would come soon enough. He had to make himself take it slowly with Roxy because of her past. It may kill him, but he would have it no other way. His eyes took in her tiny place. It was sparsely decorated, but she had made it her own because it reminded him of her with just small touches here and there.

"Hey." Her sleepy voice filled the room. "Are you okay?"

"I am," he replied. Glancing down at his cock, he frowned. He needed to take care of that before he faced her. "I needed to take a shower."

"Oh, okay." She shuffled past him, opening a door. She walked into the bathroom, and he heard her turning on the water, opening and closing doors. She stepped back out, her eyes meeting his until they dropped to his cock.

For a moment he considered covering himself but decided against it. This was him. He was a hot-blooded male who wanted his woman. She might as well get used to it.

"Can I help you with that?" she said, her voice raspy as her eyes rose to meet his.

Not much shocked him, but her words shocked the shit out of him. He had to make sure he wasn't hearing things he really wanted to hear. "What?"

Her face flushed a bright red before dropping her gaze away from him as she tried to pass him. "You better hurry before the water gets cold. The water heater here is wonky."

He grasped her arm, stopping her. "That's not what you said."

"Yes, it is." She refused to look at him. "You must still have a little bit of a fever."

He chuckled at that. "No, I'm perfectly sane at the moment." He carefully clipped her chin up so he could read her eyes. "There's nothing more that I want in this world than to make love to you, Roxy. But I'm a patient man, as I have clearly demonstrated to you, but if I heard you right and I think I did—"

"You heard me right," she whispered, trying to glance away.

"Look at me, Roxy," Marcus ordered, but without anger. "I don't want to do anything that will hurt you or make you uncomfortable."

"Sex was never an issue. It was the hitting and mental abuse that came later in my relationship with Bruce," Roxy answered without hesitation.

Marcus frowned, conflicted with emotions. Even though he was happy as hell that she wasn't afraid of sex, rage boiled through his body knowing she had enjoyed sex with someone other than him. How fucked up was that?

"I know that I shouldn't feel this way because I'm still married, but...." She shrugged, doubt flickering across her features. Her reaction brought him back to the moment.

"In my eyes, the day he laid a hand on you he was no longer your husband. I don't give a shit about a piece of paper saying otherwise. A husband never, no, a man *never* lays a hand on the woman he has sworn to protect, and that's what a husband should be." Marcus ended with a low growl, his eyes roaming her body then back up to her face. "I'm going to walk into that shower. I'm not forcing you to do anything, but if you want me, I'm here and believe me when I say, I will welcome you, protect you, and love you more than any man ever could."

He bent down and sealed his words with a hard kiss before letting her go and walking away. What he really wanted to do was rip her clothes off, carry her into the shower with him, and fuck her wet body like no one had ever fucked her before. Instead, he used every trick he could think of to calm himself from doing just that. Jesus, if she didn't come to him, he was going to have to jack off so he could walk right. He thought his shoulder hurt like a bitch; that was nothing compared to his hard-on.

\*\*\*\*\*\*

She watched him go and disappear into her small bathroom. Her last look was at his tight ass. She was horny as hell and needed him; her wet thong was a testament to that fact. Biting her lip, she glanced toward the bathroom and made an easy decision. After shedding her clothes, she walked toward the bathroom. The door was wide open, as if welcoming her. Steam rolled out, and she walked in.

"Marcus," she whispered, then cleared her throat to call his name louder, but that wasn't necessary. The curtain opened, and there he stood, his eyes intently staring into hers. "I, ah, don't like cold showers."

The smile that broke over his face was full of sensual expectation, and her nipples sprang to life as did the rest of her body. He reached out, lifted her off her feet and set her down so his body blocked most of the water. His eyes roamed down her body as they stood there, still as stone. The only sound was the water blasting his skin.

"Damn." He hissed as he ran his hands up her arms, around her neck then to her face, pulling her to him. Their bodies met at the same time their lips clashed. His hands were everywhere, and she realized so were hers. Exploring each other's bodies with a slowness that was driving her insane, she struggled to keep a coherent thought.

Once he pulled his mouth from hers, he looked down at her body again. Lowering his head so he could kiss her breast, he then took one nipple in his mouth. Her head fell back, but she didn't worry about falling with his arm wrapped around her lower back, keeping her against him. His hardness pressed against her and she swore it grew against her belly. Reaching down, she touched his tip and moaned. Not wanting to wait, she took his length in her hand, squeezing with enough pressure that he cursed. Releasing her breast, he reached around and turned off the water.

"There isn't going to be anything easy about this." He nipped her neck, then ran his tongue across it. "My control is just about gone."

"You'll get no complaints from me." She kissed his chest, moving her hand faster along his cock. His hand spread her, and she moved her leg to give him better access. One finger, then two slipped in, making her moan. She wanted more. "I'm more than ready, Marcus."

"Hell yes, you are." Marcus grabbed her hand to stop her jerking motions on his dick. "As good as your hand feels on my cock, this is going to end soon if you don't stop."

Slowly, he slipped his hand away from her pussy, down her thigh, and then hooked his large hand in the curve her knee. He picked her leg up and pressed it against his hip, opening her up wide.

Anticipation made her dizzy, but his stillness alerted her that something was wrong. Opening her eyes slowly, she saw something that she had never seen in his eyes, uncertainty. If he hadn't already had her heart, this moment would have sealed the deal.

"I want you," she whispered. "I've never been more sure of anything in my life. I want you, Marcus."

She knew he was being careful, but she didn't want anything to do with that. As he positioned himself at her opening, she used her leverage and sank onto his length in one full push. Tears pressed against her eyes, but not because of pain. No, it was because he filled her in more ways than she ever imagined could happen.

"Jesus, Roxy," Marcus said through gritted teeth. "Careful. I don't want to hurt you."

"I'm not glass." Her gasp of pleasure echoed around the small bathroom. "I won't break. Please, Marcus."

He moved inside her, slowly at first, but quickened his pace as she met him with a fervor that had them both cursing and panting. He held her close, his breath against her cheek as he pumped into her. She loved to hear him losing control. Loved the feel of his body surrounding her. She felt safe, loved and cherished.

"Grab onto my neck," he ordered, and she did quickly. When he grabbed her other leg, he lifted her, and she gladly wrapped her legs around him. With his strength, he not only pounded inside her but used his hands to control her hips. Their foreheads touched, each looking down, watching as their bodies met together in perfect rhythm. He stepped out of the tub and carefully pulled her off his length. He turned her around, his hands running from her dripping pussy, up her stomach to her breast before he bent her over. She grabbed hold of the sink with both hands as he slid inside her. His large hands gripped her hips as he once again pounded into her. "I want you every way possible," he said against her ear, his chest pressed against her back. She felt his strength as he controlled their motion.

One hand left her hip, ran up her body and squeezed one breast, pulling and twisting her nipple before doing the same to the other breast. Her breathing was so erratic she was almost afraid she was going to pass out. She knew she was close, felt her body tightening, and he must have felt it also. His hand felt its way across her stomach, stopping at the nub between her legs. He expertly worked her to the point she cried out, begging him for release. He slammed into her, their bodies slapping together loudly in the small bathroom and finally, she looked up. Their eyes met in the mirror, and she had never seen a man more intent on another's pleasure than she saw at that moment. She knew he would hold off his own pleasure until she reached hers.

Their eyes held, his hand stilled as he watched her, fucking her hard, with everything he had, and then his hand moved. With one pinch and pull, she flew over the edge, but she forced herself to keep her eyes on him. She wanted to see him release, needed to see his pleasure as he had seen hers. She screamed her pleasure, tears escaping her eyes and running down her cheeks. His head flew back, his neck corded as his mouth opened in the most erotic growl she had ever heard.

"Roxy!" She heard him, but couldn't respond. Holy shit, did she black out? "Roxy? Fuck!"

She was turned and picked up. She knew she was being carried out of the bathroom, but she couldn't open her eyes. What in the hell happened? The last thing she remembered was him with his head thrown back, mouth opened. Her pussy quivered at the memory.

"Holy shit!" she rasped out. Then she giggled as her eyes finally opened. "I think I actually blacked out."

"This isn't funny, Roxy." Marcus didn't sound happy at all. He sounded worried. "Are you okay? You went completely limp and wouldn't answer me. Jesus, did I hurt you?"

"I'm fine." Roxy leaned up, kissing him. "I swear I'm absolutely fine, but holy shit is about all I can think to say. Not very romantic, huh?" She wiped the wetness from her eyes.

Marcus finally grinned, holding her on his lap as he sat on the couch. "Holy shit pretty much sums it up."

Roxy spun around and straddled him. "Thank you." She wrapped her arms around his neck and held him tightly.

"What in the hell are you thanking me for?" Marcus ran his hands along her back. "Believe me when I say it should be me thanking the hell out of you."

"How about we just both say you're welcome and do it again?" She nipped his earlobe before sucking it in her mouth. She felt his cock swell under her. "Was that a 'you're welcome' and agreement to do it again?" she teased.

Marcus's head fell back as he laughed loudly. "That was definitely a 'you're welcome.' And me and my cock are both in total agreement." He grabbed both her tits in his hand bringing one and then the other to his mouth. "You have beautiful tits, and I could do this all fucking day."

He watched as he sucked and licked on her tits, not realizing her hips had begun to move, as if seeking something long and hard to play with.

"Sorry, are my words too vulgar?" Marcus frowned, moving his hands back to her hips.

"I like you vulgar." Roxy moaned when he ran his thumb along the crease of her pussy. "Actually, it turns me on more because your voice is sexy anyway, so when you are saying dirty things, it makes me want you more."

"Then expect some pretty fucking vulgar stuff to come out of my mouth." Marcus reached up, grabbed the back of her neck and pulled her in for a kiss. "I plan on fucking that sweet pussy of yours for the rest of the night. Did you enjoy me fucking you from behind?"

"Absolutely." Roxy found his cock with her bare pussy and rubbed against it.

"Good, because I plan on fucking you every way possible, Roxy." Marcus growled, then pulled her head back to look directly at her. "I also plan on making love to you slow and long."

"It's different?" Roxy sighed, loving this side of Marcus.

"Oh yeah, very." Marcus chuckled with a cocked eyebrow. "Very different."

"So I'd say what we just did was fuck?" Roxy enjoyed teasing him. That was one thing they'd done from the very start. Teasing each other was so comfortable for them both.

"Definitely." He nodded, his sexy grin in place.

"So, when does the making love begin because I'd really like to see what the difference is, Marcus Foster." She tried to appear innocent but knew she wasn't even close to appearing that way.

"Just as soon as you open those pretty legs of yours." He growled when she opened them further, inviting him inside.

"Jesus." He moaned, but before he could sink inside her, someone knocked loudly on the door. "Fuck!" Still holding her, he quickly stood and carried her to the bedroom.

"Who is it?" Roxy wondered out loud as he put her down.

"I don't know, but stay here," he ordered, then gazed down at her body and cursed. "It better be a fucking emergency, or I'm going to kill someone."

Roxy laughed as she watched him close the door, and waited. She heard voices and recognized Hunter. She walked over to the bed and lay on her stomach and waited, realizing she had never been happier in her life. Marcus was who she should have been with from the start, and deep inside she knew it.

Finally, the door opened, and Marcus walked in carrying clothes.

"Is Hunter still alive?" She grinned, enjoying the way his eyes roamed her naked body.

"For the moment." He tossed his clothes on the floor and stalked toward her. "Now, where were we?"

"I think you were about to show me the difference between fucking and making love." She rolled over and slowly opened her legs for him.

"If you don't stop doing things like that, the making love may have to wait a little longer," he said with a growl and crawled between her legs. "Just in case you didn't hear me before, I love you." He stared down at her, all teasing gone.

Her heart swelled, her body trembled, and a tear escaped. "I did hear, and I love you too, Marcus."

She lay back as he showed her the difference between fucking and making love. She enjoyed every moment, welcoming the bliss that came with exploring and being with Marcus. But she gave just as good as she got. There was no way she would deny this man anything, ever.

# Chapter 10

"How about a date?" Marcus asked as he and Roxy walked into town. A misty rain was beginning to fall, and fog hung low in the trees, but all he saw was her smiling face.

"A date?" Roxy chuckled. "Should that have been, you know, first? I think we're beyond the dating thing."

"Seriously." Marcus grinned down at her, then pulled the hood of her coat up, covering her head. "Tonight I'll pick you up and take you out for a nice dinner and dancing."

"Dancing?" Roxy looked up at him from under her hood. "You dance?"

"There isn't anything like dancing with a beautiful woman in your arms." Marcus winked at her.

"You are such a charmer, aren't you?" Roxy cocked her eyebrow before glancing away.

He saw a hint of concern in her eyes, but waited. He knew what her concern was and he was going to help her conquer her fears one by fucking one. "Only when I need to be," he teased. "So how about it? I pick you up at your place about seven?"

"There isn't any place here to have dinner or dance." She put her head on his shoulder. "How about I cook us dinner, and we play the radio?"

"Nope, want to take you out." His tone was stern as if he wasn't taking no for an answer.

"Marcus, I'd love to go out with you, but...." Her voice changed to uncertainty, which pissed him off.

He stopped them and turned her to face him. "No one's ever going to hurt you again." He stared into her eyes, willing her to believe him. "You've stayed in this town long enough. It's time I get to show you off to the world."

"Not much to show." She rolled her eyes, but not before he saw a spark of interest in her beautiful green eyes.

"You really don't know how beautiful you are." It wasn't a question, just a true statement. "Trust me, Roxy."

Her gaze searched his. "I do trust you," she replied, then nodded. "Okay, it's a date. Don't be late."

His smile was huge as he grabbed her to him. "Yes!"

"You're crazy." She shook her head, laughing. "Come on, I'm going to be the one late. I have coffee drinkers to take care of. They get mean when they have to wait."

"Who the hell's been mean?" His voice went instantly hard, his anger rising quickly.

"Nobody." Roxy laughed. "Calm down, killer. It's just most coffee drinkers are grumpy until after their first cup. No one has been mean to me."

"Yeah, well they better not." Marcus frowned as they walked again. "It'll be pretty hard to drink coffee when I knock out their teeth."

"Ah, okay, that made no sense." Roxy laughed loudly. "Why would not having teeth keep someone from drinking coffee?"

Once they made it to the door, he took the keys from her. "I don't know." He grinned down at her. "Just couldn't think of anything else." She laughed again, and he swore he would do everything in his power to hear her sweet laughter every chance he could, even if it meant he had to be an idiot.

After making sure the store was clear and once Clare arrived, he headed toward Garrett's. Stepping inside, he went directly to the kitchen. Sam was at the kitchen counter eating out of a large mixing bowl with Pepper, aka Max, lying next to his stool, giving Marcus the bored stare.

"What are you eating, little man?" Marcus pulled up a stool and sat down.

"Fru-Fru-Fruity Pebbles." He tilted the bowl so Marcus could see.

"The whole box?" Marcus grinned at the large bowl.

"Yup." Sam took a large tablespoon bite, then wiped the dribbling milk on his chin. "I wa-wa-want to be bi-big as you guys. So I nee-nee-needs to eat."

"You better hurry, buddy." Garrett entered, grinning at the giant bowl, but didn't say anything. "You're going to be late for school. Jenny's already sent a note home about you being late."

"I know." Sam took one more mouthful then jumped off the stool and grabbed his backpack. He collected his bowl, dumped the contents in the garbage and put the bowl in the sink. "But it is-is-isn't my fau-faul-fault. It was warm and... and... and I didn't wan-wan-wan-want to sit in that stink-stinky room."

Both men watched Sam sigh with a big heave of his shoulders before snapping his fingers for Pepper to follow him, and out the door he went. Both men started laughing.

"How many times were we late for school for the same reason?" Marcus shook his head.

"All the damn time." Garrett snorted, collecting Sam's bowl and putting it in the dishwasher.

"You've got your hands full with that one." Marcus took a drink of coffee that Roxy sent with him.

"Tell me about it," Garrett said, sounding like it was a chore, but he couldn't have looked happier. "The kid is eating us out of house and home. He thinks the more he eats, the quicker he will grow. Instead, he ate so much last night he threw up everywhere."

"Well, if Janna was cooking her gross shit, I can see why." Hunter came in at the end of Garrett's sentence and looked at Marcus. "About fucking time you got back. You finished playing house with Ms. Roxy Patel?"

"Watch it," Marcus warned with narrowed eyes. "Don't go where you're going to get your ass handed to you."

"Play house?" Garrett frowned. "I thought you were healing."

"Oh, he was healing all right," Hunter continued, ignoring the growling coming from Marcus. "I showed up there yesterday, which by the way, he was up, walking around, looking fine and dandy—"

"I have never looked fucking dandy."

"As well as answering a certain lady's door naked as the day he was born." Hunter finished with a wicked gleam in his eyes. "I'd say he was healed up nicely and decided to play hooky."

"Fucker." Marcus growled at Hunter.

"Okay, well I guess you're good enough to take some of the new shifters out tonight," Garrett said, pouring himself a cup of coffee.

"Can't," Marcus said, still glaring at Hunter. "Got a date."

"Well, la fucking da." Hunter rolled his eyes. "And I got me a woman who I haven't seen in two days while you healed."

"You're such a dick," Marcus sneered, then turned to Garrett. "If you get Dell to take tonight, I'll do the next two nights."

"I'll talk to him when he shows up, but in the meantime, we have interviews to finish up, so get your asses over to Jonah's." Garrett glanced toward the hallway that led upstairs. "I'm going to make sure Janna is good before I head over."

"How's she doing?" Marcus asked, knowing that his brother was concerned. Janna was having a hard time with the pregnancy, so they were taking every precaution they could.

"She's doing okay. Just ready to not be pregnant." He frowned, then looked at Marcus. "And we both owe Roxy our gratitude. We heard why Roxy was beating the hell out of Deb."

Marcus nodded then glanced at Hunter, who also looked angry. "Yeah, it didn't sit well with Roxy."

"It didn't sit well with Emily either." Hunter snorted, then stood. "Deb got another beatdown the next day."

"Okay, enough gossip." Garrett poured the rest of his coffee in the sink. "Get your asses out of my house. Don't you have a place of your fucking own?"

"He loves us." Hunter gave Garrett a goofy grin. "Don't ya, bro?"

"Fuck you, Hunter," Garrett said as he disappeared.

"So where you taking Rockin' Roxy?" Hunter asked, then laughed. "I always wanted to call her that."

"Yeah, well make that the last time." Marcus gave him a disapproving glare. "And somewhere in Lexington. I'm getting her the hell out of the town for the night."

"Is there gonna be…." Hunter did the circle with a finger pumping in and out of it.

"You just want me to kick your ass, don't you?" Marcus made a grab for him, but Hunter dodged. "What in the hell is wrong with you?"

"Lighten up, grumpy ass." Hunter punched him in the arm and then took off to where Emily stood by the feed mill talking to a construction worker. "I'll be there in a minute."

Marcus rolled his eyes at his brother, then grinned. Damn, he was an idiot, but he'd want no one else at his back when there was trouble. Emily glanced up and tossed him a wave with a large smile. He watched Hunter grab her and give her a kiss. He was happy they'd finally found happiness.

"Shit, I'm turning into a fucking woman," Marcus said to himself, disgusted. But deep inside, he was one happy motherfucker himself.

\*\*\*\*\*\*

Roxy finished cleaning and getting the coffee shop ready for another day. She waited for Clare to bring her some dresses she could try on to wear tonight. After agreeing to go on a date, she totally forgot she didn't have anything nice to wear. She considered canceling, but remembered how happy Marcus seemed when she'd finally agreed to go.

"Sorry!" Clare ran in out of breath. "My mom called, and I couldn't get off the phone with her."

A little bit of her excitement dimmed at the mention of Clare talking to her mom. She missed her mom and dad so much, but she couldn't chance contacting them because of Bruce. He had threatened more than once to make her family's life a living hell. It was best for them if they just forgot about her. They hadn't been happy about her marriage to Bruce and had been livid when they'd moved from California.

"Hey." Clare was in front of her, waving her hand in front of her face. "You in there?" She laughed but looked a little concerned, her eyes searching.

"Sorry." Roxy shook her head. "Zoned out for a minute. And you're fine. I just got done preparing everything for in the morning. Plus I can't leave until someone comes to walk me home."

"Do you even know how lucky you are?" Clare sighed dramatically. "Marcus Foster is... I don't even know the right words to describe that sexy piece of man meat. I should hate you, you know that."

"Why in the world would you hate me?" Roxy frowned.

"Ah, because I've lived here all my life and panted after Marcus since the day he moved here, and then here you come and bam... the man of my dreams is completely and utterly taken." Clare glared at her before bursting into laughter. "You should really see your face right now."

"You're kidding?" Roxy was really feeling upset that maybe Clare was serious. She didn't want to hurt her friend in any way.

"Yeah, I'm kidding." Clare snorted, shaking her head. "Well kinda. I mean he is one piece of hunky-ass man, but he isn't the man of my dreams, and I've never panted after a man in my life."

"He is pretty hunky." Roxy grinned, relieved that Clare had been joking with her.

"God, we sound like we're in high school." Clare turned and grabbed the dresses. "Okay, I have three dresses. I think the black one is the best for you, but I brought a blue and a green one. I have shoes also. Everything should fit. The dresses might be a little tight in the boobs, and that I am damn jealous about, not lying."

"Thank you so much, Clare." Roxy looked over the dresses, then at her friend. "And thank you for being my friend."

"You deserve happiness, Rox face." Clare used the nickname she had called her one night when they'd had a few too many drinks. "And never thank me for being your friend. I've got your back, girl."

"And I've got yours, Clare bear." Roxy grinned and gave her a tight hug.

"What the hell is going on and did you just call her Clare bear?" Hunter walked in, throwing a cursory glance at the dresses and shoes. He picked up the black one and wiggled his eyebrows. "This one is a definite and these shoes, which are to die for by the way."

"You've got good taste." Clare laughed, watching Hunter go through the clothes.

"Girl, you have no idea." Hunter dropped the shoes and crossed his arms. "I know more about women's clothing than any man."

"I really don't know how to take that other than you're weird." Clare shook her head and then headed for the door. "You have a good time tonight, Roxy. And I expect all the juicy details in the morning. Ta-ta."

"Ta-ta!" Hunter called out after her, but his eyes stayed on Roxy. "So, you and my brother, huh?"

Roxy shrugged, uncomfortable. Maybe Marcus's brothers wouldn't approve of her; she'd never thought about that. "Maybe."

"Maybe my ass." Hunter helped her gather up everything. "You guys were made for each other, and he's been in love with you since the day Garrett brought you to town."

"Really?" Roxy glanced at Hunter quickly, then away, hating the hopeful tone of her voice.

"Yeah, really." Hunter laughed. "You know the night you made Garrett dinner and he showed up with Janna? And then I came to find you to make sure you were okay?"

"Yes." Roxy wished she didn't remember it. She was humiliated and embarrassed beyond belief.

"Well, Marcus found out that Garrett sent me to find you and he about killed me, thinking I put the moves on you." Hunter gave her an "I shit you not" look. "He was pissed at Garrett for sending me after you."

A tingle low in her stomach grew until her stomach did an excited flip. "But I was fine."

"I know." Hunter grinned. "But everyone thought I was going to put my famous irresistible moves on you, which I didn't. I mean you're hot as hell, but you belonged to my brother."

"I didn't belong to your brother." Roxy walked toward the back to switch off the lights. "I didn't even know he knew who the hell I was other than saying hi. Well, at least at that time."

"Oh yeah, you did. And he knew you more than you know he knew you." Hunter noticed the odd look she was giving him. "Yeah, you know what I mean, so stop looking at me like that. Now come on, let's get out of here and get you ready for your big date."

He helped her grab her stuff and lock up. They were both quiet on their walk. She felt a little silly about having to be walked home. "I could have gotten home okay. You didn't have to walk me."

"If I value my life, I did," Hunter said without looking at her. "Plus, Marcus is buying me a case of beer."

"He's paying you to walk me home, in beer?" Roxy gave him a sideways glance.

"He doesn't know it yet, but yes," Hunter replied, his eyes scanning the area.

As much as Hunter made jokes, he was alert to his surroundings. She felt as safe with him as she did Marcus. Their whole walk she noticed he never looked at her, but remained vigilant, and only talked when spoken to, which was not normal for Hunter usually.

Once they were at her door, he took her keys. "Stay here."

She waited just inside the door as he set her shoes on the floor and walked through her house. "Okay."

"Thank you, Hunter." Roxy smiled, laying out the dresses so they didn't wrinkle. "What kind of beer do you drink? I think it's only fair since it's me you're walking that I pay you."

Hunter turned toward her, a serious look on his face. "Make my brother happy." He gave her a nod. "That's all I ask. You kids have fun tonight."

"I'm a little nervous," Roxy admitted before he could walk out the door. She didn't know why she told him. Maybe she needed to tell someone, and he was the only one available.

Hunter stopped and turned toward her. "I don't know your story, Roxy. But I pretty much figured it out without knowing all the details. I also know this will be the first time you've left town since you've been here." Hunter stepped up to her and hugged her tightly. "It's time to start living your life. Trust my brother. He'd lay down his life for you. No one will ever hurt you again."

Her chin trembled, but she refused to cry. She was sick and tired of crying, of being afraid and unsure. "I do trust him." She nodded, then gave him a shaky smile.

"I know trust is hard to come by, but there's no one better to put your trust into than Marcus." Hunter turned and opened the door, throwing over his shoulder, "Lock up," as he closed the door behind him.

She hurried to lock the door. Hunter didn't budge until the lock clicked, then he took off at a run and disappeared. Turning, she looked at the dresses and then the clock. She needed to hurry.

Excitement swirled through her body as she rushed to the shower. At that moment, she decided she would enjoy this night and think of nothing but having a good time with Marcus.

# Chapter 11

Marcus couldn't stop staring at Roxy. Holy shit, she was beautiful, and if one more man stared at her tits, he was going to explode in a fit of rage. He'd glared and growled more in the last half an hour than he had in his entire fucking life.

When she'd opened her front door to him, he was speechless. He was never speechless, but the sight of her in that tight black dress was almost too much for him to even form a single comprehensible word.

"Marcus?"

Another man passed their table, his eyes glued to Roxy, and Marcus had to stop himself from reaching out and grabbing the bastard.

"Marcus!"

"Yeah?" Marcus sneered at the man, then looked at Roxy. "I'm sorry. What?"

"We can leave if you want." She glanced at the man who was hurrying away.

"What? No!" Marcus frowned, then ran his hand through his hair. "Damn, I'm sorry."

"It's okay. It just doesn't seem like you're having a very good time." Roxy took a sip of wine. "Really, we can leave. We haven't ordered yet."

Marcus called himself every name in the book. He had sworn she would never feel disappointment at his hands, yet there he was ruining her night with his jealous raging, a night he'd talked her into. She would have been just as happy at home as she said, cooking him dinner and dancing to the radio.

"I really am sorry." Marcus felt like an ass. "It's the wolf in me. I didn't think it would be this hard."

Roxy smiled, then grabbed her wine and stood. "Then let's do this." She moved next to him as he stood and pulled out a chair. "Put it next to yours."

Marcus grinned as she sat, then he sat beside her, putting his arm around the back of her chair.

"Now, everyone will know exactly who I belong to." She kissed his cheek. "And you aren't the only one. There're a few women in here whose hair I'd like to yank out, but being I'm in a dress, I guess I need to be all ladylike."

"We are a pair." Marcus chuckled, shaking his head. Seemed like he wasn't the only one who was a little possessive and he liked it, a lot.

"That we are." Roxy picked up her glass as he picked up his beer. They clinked glasses and laughed. The waiter came and took their order, poured Roxy some more wine, and placed another beer for Marcus. "So, how was your day?"

"Long," he replied, his hand rubbing circles on her shoulder. "I didn't think it would end. I kept thinking about tonight."

"I know," Roxy agreed. "Thank you for this. I know it didn't seem like it at first, but I was really excited about coming out with you."

"You deserve to be wined and dined." Marcus's hand moved to the back of her neck. "And I plan on doing it often."

Roxy moaned as he massaged her neck. "That feels good."

"You keep moaning like that, we might have to skip dancing," he whispered in her ear before kissing her neck.

"And you would get no complaints from me," she teased with a saucy wink.

\*\*\*\*\*\*

His heated look warmed her to her soul. Just his look said so much that words weren't needed. His gaze moved to her breasts, and her nipples hardened instantly. This time he was the one that moaned. She grinned, wanting him to feel what she did, but she didn't think she could do it with just a look.

"I'm not wearing any...." She started to say, but the waiter showed up with their food. Her message was heard by Marcus loud and clear, and he moved in his seat adjusting his crotch quickly. She surprised herself by giggling.

"You're going to pay for that," he warned with a deliciously evil smile, then thanked the waiter.

"Can't wait," she countered, as she also thanked their waiter.

"You really don't have anything on under that dress?" he whispered as he cut his steak.

"No, I really don't." She grinned when his fork clattered against the plate.

"Shit!" he hissed, then adjusted himself again.

They enjoyed their dinner, neither saying much. She did notice how fast they both ate, though, and grinned.

"Keep grinning, Roxy Patel." Marcus took a long drink of his beer. "You thought I fucked you last night. That's nothing compared to what I'm going to do to you tonight." He took a big bite of steak, tearing it with his teeth and then chewed slowly as he stared at her.

She had a full mouth, swallowed hard and almost choked. She felt the wetness between her legs and prayed she wasn't going to have a large wet spot on the back of her dress, on Clare's dress. Looking down at her half-eaten food, she was suddenly full, her appetite for food completely gone. Dabbing her mouth, she placed her napkin next to her plate.

"That was good," she said, clearing her throat.

"You finished?" Marcus's voice was deep and low, sending shivers throughout her body.

"Yes." She smiled with a blush.

"Dessert?" He leaned forward and whispered for her ears only.

She leaned in toward him, her smile fading slightly. "Definitely."

His eyes darkened, nostrils flared as he waved the waiter down for their check. As they waited and not very patiently, Marcus put his large hand on her thigh, asserting just enough pressure as he moved it closer to the part that throbbed for him.

"I can smell you." He closed his eyes for a second before opening them to look down her body. "You want me."

Heat flashed across her face, and she wished they were anywhere but sitting in a crowded restaurant. With just her eyes, she glanced around. No one paid them any attention. Her eyes returned to him, then down to his lap. "I can see *you.*" She smiled slowly as she looked back up into his eyes. "You want *me.*"

"Oh, if you only knew." Marcus's laugh warmed her; it was genuine and made her feel special. "It's going to be a trick walking out of here without my dick knocking people over."

A loud laugh escaped her, drawing attention to them. She covered her mouth quickly but couldn't stop laughing.

"Hey, it's big and hard enough." He frowned as if offended that she was laughing so hard. "I'll have you know my manhood has claimed many victims."

"Stop," she wheezed, shaking her head. "I can't breathe." She picked her napkin up to dab her eyes as the waiter dropped off their check. Marcus watched her as he pulled his wallet out of his back pocket and laid out cash on the table. She had often wondered what he and his brothers did for money but never asked, despite her curiosity.

"You ready?" He stood and pulled her chair out. He helped her into her jacket, then led her toward the front of the restaurant with his hand on her lower back.

She loved when he did that. A man stood in front of them, then quickly moved to let them pass. She tried to control the giggle that escaped her lips.

"That was a close call," Marcus whispered in her ear as they passed. "I thought the poor bastard was a goner."

Roxy laughed again and tried to control it until they were outside. Once at the car, he removed his keys and clicked the fob. The lights flashed and the doors unlocked. Before opening her door, he turned her, pressing her against the car and kissed her. She knew without a doubt she was going to be okay because she wanted his kiss more than anything, waited for it, prayed for it, and almost did it her damn self. But she was glad she had been patient; it was so worth it.

He pulled away and smiled down at her. "I've wanted to do that all night."

"What took you so long?" She sighed, opening her eyes slowly.

He turned serious, his eyes narrowing slightly. "I wanted to wait until we were here so you would have a better memory of parking lots."

His words broke and mended her heart all at the same time. A single tear slipped down her cheek. "Are you real?" she whispered, searching his face.

Surprise flickered in his eyes before it was gone. He leaned close to her ear as he moved her so he could open her door. "You're going to find out how real I am, very soon."

He helped her slide into the car, then closed the door. Her moment alone allowed her to place her hand on her heart and close her eyes. "Wow," she whispered, then reached up and wiped another tear that escaped. She then pinched her arm to make damn sure she wasn't dreaming. The pain clearly telling her this was no dream.

******

Marcus did his best not to shove his hand up Roxy's dress to see if she really was bare. Damn, she gave as good as she got. She might blush, but that didn't stop her from saying and doing what she wanted.

He had figured with dinner and dancing it would be too late to drive back to Beattyville so he'd reserved them a room. He'd never been more relieved to have planned ahead. Pulling into the parking lot, he found a close parking spot and turned off the car, glancing at Roxy who had a half grin on her face.

Marcus got out of the car with a grin of his own, hurried to her side and opened the door. His eyes skimmed over her legs and she carefully got out of the car. As far as he was concerned, there was nothing sexier than a woman in a short dress and high heels. He took her hand in his and silently they walked inside and to the front desk.

"Mr. Foster." The man behind the desk beamed at them. "Your room is ready. If you can just sign, you're good to go."

"Thanks, Fred." Marcus signed, took the key, grabbed her hand and headed for the elevator.

"Come here much?" Roxy gave him a sideways glance.

Marcus only smiled, then pushed the button on the elevator. Once inside, he leaned against one side while Roxy went to the other. A woman stepped in and hit a button. The doors closed, and the elevator music broke the silence. Marcus stared at Roxy, his eyes devouring her. She stared right back, not even looking away when the doors opened, and the woman walked out. The doors closed again, but still, they remained silent, their gazes locked. If she only knew what was in store for her, he thought as a wicked grin slipped across his lips.

The doors opened and he reached out, clasping her arm and escorting her out. Once at the door, he opened it, and she gasped.

"It's beautiful." She looked around and his gaze followed. The windows in the top suite had a stunning view of the mountains. The huge full moon hung low in the sky. He couldn't have asked for a better view for her.

He glanced at the table and was relieved that his orders had been followed. Walking over, he flipped on the radio and was happy hard metal music didn't blare from the speakers. He turned toward her. She stood looking out the large window, but turned at the sound of the music.

They met in the middle of the room. He took her into his arms. "I told you there would be dancing." He pressed her against him, their bodies swaying.

"Yes, you did." Roxy smiled against his chest.

Even as the music stopped and another song began, they kept swaying. Slowly, he inched her dress up, his fingers touching her bare ass. "You weren't lying." He cupped her cheek, giving it a squeeze.

Before she could respond, he took her mouth with his. Their tongues slowly tangled. He wanted to make this night special for her, so he made damn sure he remained in complete control of his wolf, not easy for a shifter with a healthy appetite for sex, especially sex with his mate.

"You want some wine?" he whispered, reluctantly removing his hand from her bare skin.

Roxy looked up at him and shook her head. "No. I want to remember this night clear-headed."

As the second song ended, the next started and Marcus removed his shoes, kicking them aside. He then undid his belt and black slacks, and tugged on his boxers, letting them fall to the floor before stepping out of them. His large hands grasped her hips and slowly, he picked her up, making sure her dress slipped up, baring her pussy. The red triangle of hair made him groan. Angling his hips, he lowered her onto his hard cock until they were one. He continued to sway with the music as she wrapped her arms around his neck, their eyes focused on each other.

He smiled when she moved against him. She wanted him, but he used his strength to keep her in place not allowing her to move. "Not until after this dance," he said against her lips.

"Please," she whispered back before sucking his lower lip between hers.

He pulled a hairbreadth away. "No, I promised you dancing, so we'll finish this dance," he teased, loving the feel of her against him.

She leaned back, her breasts straining against the thin black material of her dress. Her pert nipples begged to be sucked. Not wanting to disappoint them, he took one between his teeth and bit down easy. Her moans turned him on more than anything could. To know he was pleasuring his mate was what he lived for, what any wolf shifter lived for.

The song finished, another began. With a tight grip on her ass and thighs, he pulled her off his length and pushed her back on slowly.

"Bare them," he ordered, his eyes on her tits. She did as he asked, the dress being pulled to the side, pushing her tits together. He took one in his mouth and sucked as he continued the slow motion of fucking her.

"I could have taken it off." Roxy's words were raspy with desire.

"No fucking way." Marcus growled. "When I first saw you in this dress I knew I'd be fucking you with you still in it. Don't ruin my dirty thoughts."

He looked down to watch his cock slide in and out of her tight, wet pussy. It was the most erotic thing he had ever seen. He sped up, then slowed down, over and over again. Lifting his gaze, he saw Roxy watching also with a look of pleasure he had never seen on a woman's face before. He almost blew his fucking load then and there.

Knowing this was not going to last as long as he had wanted it to, he made his way toward the wall. He needed leverage so he could pound her.

"Seems like I'm failing miserably at making love to you." He gritted his teeth when she rubbed her pelvis against him. Her breaths coming in small gasps.

"Perfect." Roxy sighed, then began bouncing up and down, but he stopped her.

Realizing that there was a ledge running the length of the window, he headed that way instead and pulled her off him. Turning her around, he bent her over as she grabbed on to the ledge. She quickly spread her legs apart for him, and he gave a masculine grin. He flipped the dress up, baring her ass. Taking his cock in his hand, he slid easily into her. Seeing her head was down, he reached out and gently grabbed her hair to pull her head back as he fucked her hard, slow, and every way in between. "Enjoy the view, Roxy."

# Chapter 12

Roxy lay in the bed that felt like a cloud. She was on her side watching Marcus sleep and wondered if she was being creepy. Probably, but she didn't care. Last night was magical. She knew that sounded corny as hell, but again she didn't care. It had been amazing, and she would never forget it. No man had ever taken care of her like Marcus had. Not only physically, but emotionally.

Her eyes ran down his muscular and strong body. His tan made her look so pale against him. She sighed, her eyes traveling back up to see him staring at her.

"Sorry." She blushed. "I was being creepy and watching you sleep."

"That's okay. I did the same thing for about an hour after you fell asleep." He grinned, then stretched and flexed before rolling toward her.

"We're pathetic." She laughed, slapping her hand on her forehead.

He shrugged, then reached out to move a strand of hair out of her eyes. "Pathetic, creepy, who cares?"

"Right, who cares?" she agreed, then bit her lip. "Can I ask you a question?"

"You can ask me anything." Marcus rose, putting his head on his hand to peer down at her.

"Do you come here often? The man at the desk seemed to know you pretty well." She felt silly for asking, but curiosity got the better of her. "I mean I don't care or anything. I was just wondering."

"Yes, I've been here a few times," he responded, watching her intently.

"Oh." Okay, she'd said she didn't care, but why did she feel so disappointed with his answer. She knew he had to have been with plenty of women. Seriously, with his looks that was a no-brainer.

"Oh?" Marcus clipped her chin up to look at him. "That's all you've got to say?"

"Yes, pretty much," she said, then frowned. "Well, no, not really. I really don't care how many women you've been with in your past. But I'm a little disappointed that you brought me to a place you've had other women. I know I probably shouldn't feel that way, but I guess I do."

"Thank you for being honest. It's so damn refreshing." Marcus smiled down at her. "And I've never brought a woman here. I come to Lexington for business regularly, and I like this room. I don't feel closed in because of the windows and view. I wanted to share it with you."

"Oh." Roxy replied, relieved. He liked honesty, so he'd get honest. "I'm glad. So what kind of business or is that rude of me to ask?"

"I've fucked you every which way, Roxy. I think you have a right to know a little about me." Marcus kissed her cheek. "My mother was human, and my father was alpha. After they had us, my mother was not happy being a shifter's wife, especially the wife of an alpha. We had met her mother, our grandmother, a few times a year. She was such an awesome little woman and loved us. My mother finally left our father, and our father drank himself to death."

"How sad." Roxy touched his arm. "I'm so sorry, Marcus."

"It happens." He shrugged, but she saw the pain in his eyes before he hid it. "A few years later a lawyer found us. It seemed our grandmother left us an inheritance. I went to college, learned about stocks and investing. Taught my brothers what I knew and we invested in both stocks and real estate. We've done pretty well for ourselves."

"Yes, you have." Roxy agreed, looking around the beautiful suite. "You don't flash your money. I've never seen that Mustang GT you drove here in before, and I have no idea where you live. So, I was just curious how you could afford this place. I'm sorry if that was nosy of me."

"Anything you want to know about me, ask me. I have nothing to hide from you, Roxy. And I have two places actually." Marcus used his fingertip to trace the outline of her lips. "One that I built for my mate. I've never stayed there. The other one I live in. It's small, but does the job for me."

"Why don't you live in the one you built?" Roxy asked, confused.

"Because we build in hopes of finding our mate, but we don't live there, not until our mate walks in the door with us." Marcus moved from her lips to her nose. "It's the shifter way."

"That's really nice," Roxy said and meant it. Tradition seemed lost in the world today, but the shifters seemed to keep them.

"I'm hoping that my mate approves of what I've built and decides to live with me soon." Marcus stared at her nose as his finger traced along it.

"Have you asked her or... him?" Roxy laughed loudly when he quickly climbed on top of her, holding her arms to the bed.

"Him?" He narrowed his eyes at her. "Have I given you the impression I'm gay?"

"No." She shook her head. "It's just Hunter said once that—"

"Hunter's an idiot and needs his ass kicked," Marcus grumbled. "But no, I have not asked *her* yet. Still have a few finishing touches before it's ready."

"Well, I'm sure she'll be very happy with it." Roxy wiggled underneath him. She'd live in a tent if he'd ask her, that she knew for a fact. She was totally, 100 percent in love with this man.

"She better be." He growled and swooped in for a kiss, but the loud ringing of his phone stopped him. "Shit! I have to get that. It's Garrett's ring."

Roxy nodded, her eyes going to his ass as he stood naked and answered his phone.

"Yeah." Marcus's deep voice had a unique way of soothing her. "Okay. I'll be there in an hour. Okay. Later."

"Everything okay?" Roxy sat up, holding the covers to her chest.

Marcus frowned, walking to her side of the bed. "Have to take a raincheck on the rest of the day. I need to get back."

"That's fine." Roxy reached up and pulled him down for a kiss, hiding her disappointment. "Thank you for last night. I'll never forget it."

"It's one of many we will have, Roxy." Marcus winked at her then whipped the covers away. His eyes roamed her body. "Damn! I can't believe I'm going to say this, but we need to get dressed and on the road."

Roxy chuckled when he looked at her once again and moaned as if in pain before walking away. She hurried to dress, which took her all of two seconds. She went into the bathroom, cleaned up, and checked her appearance in the mirror. Frowning, she fluffed her shoulder-length hair and used her fingers to tease it a bit, then sighed. She had always wondered how women in movies and television shows always looked amazing when they woke up. Glam crew, she rolled her eyes. Something she would never have.

Opening the door, her gaze landed on Marcus who leaned against the wall waiting for her. "Damn, you look even more beautiful than you did last night."

"Keep that up, Mr. Foster, and I might keep you around for a while." Roxy winked, then squealed when he grabbed her up against him.

"Honey, you don't have a choice." He nipped her neck. "I'm not going anywhere."

\*\*\*\*\*\*

Marcus grinned as he backed out of Roxy's long driveway. Soon, she would be living with him, and he couldn't wait. He hated leaving her there alone; it drove him nuts. Hell, a fucking kid could kick in the doors. It was an old house that had seen many years. Once on the main road, he drove the short trip to Jonah's. Once there, he climbed out of the car and glanced toward all the construction going on, his eyes searching for what he didn't know, but just hearing that Roxy's ex owned a construction company made him a little edgy.

Pushing it aside for now, he knocked once then walked in. "What's up?"

Jonah frowned, his eyes going to Ross who sat glaring at her phone. "Ask her."

"This." She held up her phone, showing pictures.

Marcus looked at the phone, flipping through the pictures, his anger growing with each photo. In each, Carl stood behind someone in their town, just close enough that he could be seen on camera. The next picture froze his soul. It was Roxy taking the garbage out the back of the coffee shop. The fucker was leaning against a tree with a sadistic grin on his face, looking straight at the camera.

"Motherfucker." Marcus gave the phone back to Ross.

"I second that," Ross said with a frown. "He's crazy. This is just a warning, proving he can get close to anyone in this town and no one can do anything about it."

Leda ran in at that moment. "Pepper's missing," she said, her face pinched with worry. "Sam's freaking out. That dog is never two steps away from him."

"It's him." Ross stood and headed for the door.

"Go get Roxy and take her to Garrett's," he ordered Jonah, hating the fact he couldn't do it himself. Though he trusted Jonah and knew he would fight to the death, he only really trusted himself to keep her safe.

"On it." Jonah was out the door with Marcus hot on his heels.

Marcus took off toward the woods where he saw Ross shift and disappear. In seconds, he shifted, clearing his mind to let his wolf take over. If that bastard hurt Sam's dog, he was dead. No, the fucker was dead for the threat he'd made by taking a picture of his mate.

Once he was further in the woods, Marcus sensed Hunter, Garrett, and Dell, and headed their way. Something caught his attention, and he stopped. A low whimper to his left had his wolf lifting his head and sniffing the air. Taking off in a leap, he headed that way until the whimper grew louder. He slowed and stalked, totally alert to his surroundings.

Hearing Hunter yelling had him bursting through the brush and leaping off a large rock. Hunter had shifted and was lifting Pepper in the air, a rope tied around the dog's neck. Shifting, Marcus ran to help. He quickly got the rope from around the dog's neck and checked him for injuries.

"She's okay," Marcus said, his eyes finally looking around. "What a sick fuck." The bastard had wrapped a rope around Pepper's neck and put her on a small stack of rocks. How in the hell Pepper didn't step off the rocks and hang herself was beyond him.

Pepper whimpered again, and Marcus knelt down, double-checking to make sure she was okay.

"He's gone." Dell ran up, his eyes narrowed in anger. "I have a feeling this is just the beginning."

Unfortunately, Marcus agreed. Sometimes he hated the dangers of the shifter world. It was not an easy life. "You're okay, girl." He rubbed . Pepper's head. "Come on. Let's get you back to Sam."

As they headed back to Garrett's, Marcus knew that Leda was right. Sam and Pepper were never apart. Where you could find one, the other was right there. Fear gripped him hard. The bastard could have taken Sam as well. He glanced over at Garrett who turned to look at him and knew he was thinking the same thing.

Because they were naked, they headed through the woods to the back of Garrett's house. They went in through the basement, grabbing sweats to put on quickly. Pepper was already heading up the steps. Marcus figured she was anxious to get back to Sam.

He then heard the happy scream of Sam and the excited barking of Pepper. Marcus climbed the steps, his eyes searching for Roxy. He found her smiling as she watched Sam and Pepper reunite. Their eyes met, and she walked his way.

"Are you okay?" She frowned, looking him over.

At that moment, his life was complete. He'd never had anyone worry or care about him when he came home, not that this was his home, but that was beside the point. This beautiful creature cared for him. "I am now." She went into his arms so easily, and it felt right.

# Chapter 13

Roxy and Clare were busy at work, but her mind kept going back to her night away with Marcus. Since then, he'd been really busy, so she had barely seen him. She readily admitted to herself that she missed him like crazy. After Pepper was found the previous day, patrols had been organized, and guards had been assigned to the women. Jonah had been at the coffee shop all day but had disappeared when his phone went off.

Marcus had made her stay in town at Garrett and Janna's with him. They had stayed in one of the spare bedrooms. He had gotten up early and woke her with a kiss and to tell her goodbye. She could really get used to that. It was almost five, and she was ready to go home, shower, and see Marcus. They had decided to stay open later because of the shift changes with the construction workers. It helped the crew, plus it made money for the coffee shop, so a win-win situation for all of them.

"Stop looking so down in the dumps." Clare brought in some more dishes. "Isn't he coming by later?"

"I'm fine." Roxy rolled her eyes. "I just hate doing dishes."

"Liar." Clare snorted before leaving, then stopped. "Oh, and Marcus way overpaid me for that dress. I take it he liked it."

"Very much." Roxy chuckled. Hearing the door buzz, she rinsed her hands, grabbed a towel and dried them off before heading out to help Clare. It was construction shift time.

Soon she was too busy to miss Marcus. Okay, that was a lie. She still missed him, but being busy helped. Clare took orders while Roxy filled them. Turning to hand one of the workers their orders, it dropped from her hand, crashing to the floor. Standing in front of her was Bruce.

"Hello, Roxy." His voice sent fear down her spine. Her mind shut off as her body got ready to flee.

"Look who I found." Sadie stepped up to the counter, patting Bruce on the arm.

"What are you doing here?" Roxy finally found her voice and ignored Sadie. Her heart beat so hard she seriously thought she was going to have a heart attack. Her legs felt weak, but she stood strong. She had no choice. He would not control her.

"Roxy?" Clare touched her arm. "Are you okay. You're so pale."

"What are you doing here?" Roxy's voice grew stronger. Shock and fear started to turn to anger. "If it's not to sign the divorce papers, then you can turn around and leave right now."

"Ah, shit." Clare frowned, then glared at Bruce. "That's your ex."

"Unfortunately, yes." Finally, her senses started to fire, and her eyes narrowed toward Sadie. "You're just full of games, aren't you, bitch."

The construction workers still in the shop had become very quiet until she said that. At Roxy's words, an echo of damns and chuckles spread around the room.

Bruce leaned over the counter toward her. "Watch yourself, Roxy," he sneered quietly. "I came here for honorable reasons, but that can change real quick."

She forced herself not to step back away from the threat, and he definitely was a threat no matter what he said. She had fallen for his bullshit so many times, but not anymore. "You need to leave." Thank God her voice stayed strong and clear. When he stood glaring at her, with his threatening stance leaning toward her, she knew nothing had changed. "Leave!" she shouted, pointing toward the door.

Bruce reacted so fast, he was behind the counter and pulling her toward the back. He pushed her in front of him, and she slammed into the table before she knew what was happening.

"I tried to be nice." He growled the words at her, then looked around then behind him. Grabbing her arm, he headed for her office, shoved her inside and locked the door. "I tried to be fucking nice," he yelled, his spit spraying her face.

Voices were outside the door, followed by pounding and Clare yelling like a crazy woman. "You don't know the meaning of nice." She tried to straighten, but he pushed her and held her down on the desk.

"I hear you've been whoring with a goddamn nasty shifter," Bruce spat. "What the fuck is wrong with you? We're still married."

"I stopped being your wife the first time you hit me." Tears welled in her eyes, but she fought them off. She'd be damned if she cried in front of this bastard. He wasn't worth her tears. The pounding on the door grew, and she prayed someone would break through.

Bruce glanced behind him at the door, then at the window behind her desk before looking back at her. "Listen and listen good." He grabbed her by the throat, twisting her head to face him. "You're my fucking wife, and you'll always be my fucking wife. I'm going to leave here, but you *will* return to California. I expect you there in a week. Do you understand me, bitch?"

God, she hated when he asked her that like he expected her to answer truthfully. No, she didn't understand why he did or said anything when he was in this state of mind. And he expected her to just hop on a plane for California, in a week. He was out of his damn mind, and she almost said just that, but felt it safer to remain silent. When she didn't answer and stared blankly at him, he slapped her across the face. Still, she remained silent.

"You'll go to your parents and wait for me. If I show up and you're not there, they will pay. I will ruin their lives, and you know I can fucking do it, know I *will* do it." Bruce let go of her throat and pushed away from her. "Do you even know how much money I've lost because of you. I lost my business, everything. I lost it all because of you. How dare you leave me!"

How dare she leave him? What in the hell was wrong with him? Like she owed him. Yeah, well fuck that. "How dare I leave you?" Roxy sneered, pushing herself up. "How dare you fucking beat me, control me and blame me for your failures!" she screamed, but it came out rough and raw. "I refuse to let you—"

"You refuse me nothing!" Rage consumed his voice, making his eyes bulge and face a deep shade of red. Fear trickled through her; she had never seen him so angry. "I've spent every dime I have searching for you, my fucking whore of a wife who's spreading her legs for a shifter. You're sick! And even with all that money I spent on private investigator after private investigator, it took some chick who hates you to tell me where you were and what you were up to."

Roxy continued to pray for the door to break down. For someone to rush in. She prayed for Marcus. "No, I'm not. You're the sick one, you bastard," she responded, bracing herself for the hit that she knew would follow. His fist slammed into her, knocking her off the desk and onto the floor.

"You think I'm playing a game here?" Bruce stood over her. "I have nothing to lose. You're mine and will spend the rest of your life making it up to me. You can count on that."

"Marcus will kill you." Roxy spat blood on the floor.

Bruce looked at the window again, then grabbed a chair to put under the doorknob when it looked like the door was going to burst open from all the pounding.

"And if he doesn't, I will." Roxy started to stand, fire burning through her veins. She had been through too much to go back, fought too hard, been too terrified. No more. It had to stop. "If I came back to you, I'd kill you." Hardness coated her words. "I'm not the same scared woman you knew." With a tensing of her jaw, and the need to protect herself driving her actions, she grabbed the scissors on her desk and stabbed him in the shoulder.

Bruce's howl of pain hurt her ears, but she twisted the scissors. He backhanded her across the face, sending her into the wall. Her ears rang, and black spots flashed across her eyes. All she could do was throw her hands up to defend the hell that was about to rain down on her.

\*\*\*\*\*\*

Marcus was working with the new shifters and missed the hell out of Roxy. He hadn't seen her since early that morning. "Okay, guys let's call it a day. Later tonight, shift and work in teams to run the perimeter of town. One team hide, the other team finds them. Do it over and over again. This is part of keeping our town safe and in our control from other shifters."

They headed back to town, Ross looking at her phone with a frown. He'd been impressed with her so far. She would be good for their pack. She was strong, smart, and damn fast.

"Anything from your stepbrother?" Marcus asked, his eyes scanning the area.

"Nope and that worries me." Ross put her phone in her pocket. "A silent Carl is a dangerous Carl."

They had just exited the woods and walked into town. His eyes automatically went to the coffee shop. "What the fuck?" He watched five construction workers running inside. He took off, busting through the door, but no one was in front. That was when he heard the pounding and yelling. Jumping the counter, he pushed his way through the crowd of men.

"Oh God." Clare saw him. "He's in there with her and has the door jammed."

Knocking men out of the way, he positioned himself in front of the door. "Get the fuck out of the way." He lifted his foot and kicked, but the door didn't move. "Son of a bitch." He backed up, then kicked his ass in gear using his shoulder as a battering ram. He and the door smashed into the small office.

He expected to see Carl. Instead, he saw a man he'd never seen before hovering over Roxy with his fist raised. She cowered on the floor with her hands and arms protecting herself the best she could. An inhuman roar erupted from his throat before he grabbed the man and threw him into the wall furthest from Roxy.

"You fucking dare put your hands on my mate!" Marcus thundered, his hands wrapping around the man's throat. "Who the fuck are you?"

"Her husband," the man wheezed, his face turning purple.

"She has no husband, you piece of shit," Marcus hissed then head-butted him, knocking him out cold. He let go, sending him falling to the ground. "Get my brothers!" he ordered to anyone and everyone.

When no one seemed to move, his anger swelled as his eyes fell on Roxy who half lay and half sat on the floor. Clare was checking on her. He turned to see everyone staring at Roxy, and his rage doubled. "Now!" he roared.

Kneeling, he gently moved Clare out of the way. "Baby." His body tensed seeing her hands still raised in defense. When he touched her, she flinched, and it took everything he had not to leave her and kill the bastard. But there was time for that later. She was his priority at that very moment. "Roxy, it's me. Come on, lower your arms. I don't want to hurt you."

She finally lowered her arms and looked at him with blank eyes that were slowly clearing. Her eyes shifted over his shoulder and widened. As if ashamed, she covered her face from prying eyes. "Don't touch me." Her voice cracked.

Glancing over his shoulder, he saw people staring through the doorway. "Get them the fuck out of here, Clare."

Clare stood quickly, and he heard her telling people to leave. Soon after, nothing but silence surrounded him as he stared down at the beaten woman who held his heart. His wolf raged inside him. His mind was about to explode with fury, and all he could do was sit there helpless.

"Son of a bitch." Garrett's voice filled the silence. Marcus heard his brother come up behind him, but couldn't take his eyes off Roxy.

"Get him the fuck out of here. I'll deal with him later," Marcus said, his voice flat with controlled rage.

"Is she okay?" Clare whispered, tears in her voice. "I'm so sorry. It all happened so fast. I didn't know where Jonah was and—"

"I'm fine," Roxy said from behind her hands. "I just need a minute."

Relief at hearing her voice swept through Marcus. A minute was all he was giving her. Then he glanced up at Clare. "What do you mean you didn't know where Jonah was?"

"He was gone." Clare looked down at Roxy. "And I should have sent someone to find you, but I really didn't know what to do. All I could think of was getting her out of that room, but we couldn't get the door open."

"Clare, I'm fine." Roxy finally dropped her hands from her face. "Like you said, it happened so fast it wouldn't have mattered."

Clare nodded, then slowly walked out of the room. Marcus stared at her face and never wanted to kill anyone as badly as he wanted to kill the bastard who'd damaged her. Her face was swollen, her eye already turning black. Blood trickled out one of her nostrils, and the corner of her lip was cracked.

Marcus helped her stand, pulling her into his arms. "I'm sorry...."

She gave him a small push, her face and voice hard. "I'm done being a victim." She walked around him, opened one of her drawers and pulled out some papers. "Where is he?"

"Roxy...." Marcus didn't like the idea of her going anywhere near that fucker. "Give them to me, and I'll—"

"No!" Roxy sneered, then grimaced and touched her lip. "No, where is he?"

He clasped her arm and led her out of the office, through the back room and to the front where Garrett was escorting the piece of shit out the door. "Garrett, wait," Marcus called out. Then, against his better judgment, he released her arm but stayed close to her.

She headed toward Garrett who was holding a dazed Bruce, but she veered off course and headed to where Clare and Sadie were arguing. Without stopping, she shoved Clare out of the way and punched Sadie in the mouth, hard. Sadie fell back onto one of the tables that tipped over from her weight. Both the table and Sadie crashed to the floor.

"Holy shit." Hunter quickly stepped out of Roxy's way as she headed toward him. "Were you a fighter in the past? Damn."

If Marcus wasn't so concerned about her facing her ex, he would have been damn impressed, but his focus was on what was going on now. He wished to hell he knew what the fuck was about to happen. When she walked straight up to the bastard and kicked him in the balls, even he cringed, but son of a bitch, he was definitely impressed and one proud motherfucker.

# Chapter 14

Satisfaction couldn't even describe the feeling she had at watching Bruce grabbing his balls and rolling on the floor as he moaned and gasped with pain. Tossing the papers and a pen on his face, she knelt next to him. She wasn't going to lie, she was terrified, but she was going to take her life back and end her victim status once and for all. Today it ended. She knew Marcus stood behind her, along with Garrett, Hunter, and some others. They had her back, and that was all she needed to know to have the added courage not to cower in the corner anymore. That part of her life was over.

"Sign the papers." Her voice was loud and strong. When he continued to moan and hold his balls, her anger spiked. "Sign the goddamn papers!"

"No," he answered on a pained moan, but his words were clear enough.

"If you don't sign the papers now, I will kill you," Roxy threatened. "I won't have anyone else do it and believe me when I say, there are many here that would do it, you piece of shit."

"I'll do it," Hunter volunteered, raising his hand.

"The fuck you will." Marcus growled with a fierceness that even sent a chill down her spine. "He's mine."

"I'm alpha and outrank all you fuckers," Garrett added, his tone angry.

Roxy never thought of herself as a mean person, but as Bruce finally let go of his balls to push himself up enough to look at each man who spoke and fear flooded his features, she smiled with satisfaction. "I made friends, Bruce." Roxy picked up the pen and held it out. "And I'm taking my power back today. Sign the papers."

"You're my wife." His voice didn't sound as certain now. It actually sounded whiny.

"The fuck she is." Marcus took a step, but Roxy put her hand on his leg to stop him.

She used her foot to nudge the papers toward him. "Sign."

She watched Bruce look up past her, terror registering on his face, and she wondered what Marcus was doing, but she didn't turn to look. This needed to be her doing; at least, she had to think it was her doing. Finally, he grabbed the papers, signed, and threw them at her. Roxy looked them over and frowned.

"You forgot this." She sat the papers in front of him and pointed to the blank line that required his signature.

He gripped her hand, his eyes begging her along with his pathetic words. "Don't do this, Roxy. I promise I'll—"

She started to panic when she pulled and he wouldn't release her and squeezed her hand tighter. She was getting ready to kick him when Marcus reached down, grabbed his wrist and bent it in a weird way. "Touch her again, motherfucker, and you won't be signing anything."

Roxy stopped herself from scooting away from Bruce when she was released. No, she was in control. Not him.

"You broke my wrist." Bruce was almost in tears.

"Use your left hand." Roxy offered no sympathy. How many times had she thought he broke *her* wrist.

She watched him sign, grasped the papers, and stood. Garrett reached down and seized Bruce, lifting him to his feet. "I've got him until you're ready," he told Marcus.

"Let him go." Roxy folded the divorce papers.

"What?" Marcus didn't sound happy, but she expected him not to.

She walked up to Bruce and got in his face. "If you ever come near me again, I'll kill you. I'm putting a restraining order on you. Even though I know that doesn't protect me, at least if I ever see you anywhere near me again and I do kill you, I have it on record that you're a piece of shit who needed to die. I'll be getting my concealed carry permit, so you have been warned. That's more than you ever did for me. I'm also calling the police in my parents' hometown about your threats against my parents. Just for that threat to my parents, I should let them kill you. You understand me, bitch?" She threw the hated words he had said to her for so many years in his face.

Roxy started to turn away but noticed Garrett and Marcus sending some kind of secret messages with their eyes, which pissed her off. "I mean it, Marcus." Roxy turned toward him. "I want him released. If I ever find out you or anyone here killed him, I'll leave this town, and you'll never see me again. This is what I want. This is me taking my life back, and you killing him will help you, but harm me."

She watched Marcus battle with her words, but she meant every single one. She didn't want Marcus killing her ex. Bruce wasn't worth what could happen. Bruce had a family, and they'd definitely notice he was missing. If she killed him, she would have a fighting chance. If Marcus killed him and they traced Bruce back here, it wasn't worth the risk. No, this was how she wanted it. She had to be in control of this, or she would never truly get her life back.

"Promise me." She went a step further, knowing that if Marcus promised her, he would not break it.

Marcus's eyes glared at her, his anger visible, palpable. After a few stressful seconds, he leaned closer to her. He growled his answer, "I promise," then walked away from her and toward Bruce. "Today is your lucky day, motherfucker. The only reason you're leaving this town alive is because of her and honestly, you don't deserve that kind of mercy, especially from Roxy. Any man who raises a hand to a woman is a pussy and deserves to die. I'll also promise you something, you piece of shit."

Roxy strained to hear Marcus, but the more he said, the quieter he got. He leaned closely into Bruce, whose eyes widened with fear.

"If I ever see you again, I don't even care if you are driving through this area years from now, I *will* kill you. I'll hunt you down." Marcus backed up and spat at Bruce's feet. "I'd advise you to take an alternate route."

Garrett waited until Marcus was done before shoving Bruce out the door. She started to head toward Marcus, who still had his back to her but stopped when she heard Sadie's angry voice as she finally came around and was picking herself off the ground.

"You bitch," she cried, holding the side of her face. "How dare you hit me."

"I knocked your ass out." Roxy headed her way, but Hunter stepped between them.

"Now, ladies." Hunter held his hands up.

"Get out of my way." Roxy pushed him, but he refused to budge, so she leaned over to see Sadie and pointed at her over his shoulder. "How dare I? You knew exactly what you were doing bringing my ex here, and if you don't walk your ass out of here, I'm going to knock you out again."

"I didn't do anything," Sadie said, her innocent act glaringly obvious.

"Yes, you did." Jonah walked into the shop, then turned toward Marcus. "She told me that you sent her here to get me. Said you found Carl and to head for the ridge. Garrett just told me what happened. I'm sorry, Marcus."

Marcus didn't say anything, just nodded at Jonah. But then he turned his attention back to Sadie. "I suggest you pack your shit and leave."

"Excuse me?" Sadie looked shocked.

"You heard me." Marcus turned toward Hunter, not even looking Roxy's way. "Do not leave here until I get back."

"You can't do that. I've lived here all my life," Sadie yelled, pointing at Marcus's departing back. Sadie headed for the door, her anger heating her cheeks and twisting her features. "You best watch your back," she threw at Roxy.

Roxy rolled her eyes, then sank down into a chair with a sigh. Her nerves were shot, and her face hurt, but she was damned proud of herself. She had dreamed of standing up to Bruce but never planned to hurt the one person who truly cared for her. And she knew she had hurt Marcus, or at least pissed him off enough to walk away from her. Glancing up, she saw Hunter looking at her, a strange look on his face.

"You sure know how to clear a room." Hunter cocked his eyebrow at her. "He'll be back. Just give him a minute to calm the fuck down. You took something from him that he needs to deal with."

"I couldn't let him kill Bruce, Hunter." A tear leaked from her eye, trickling down her sore cheek. "Not over me. I know Bruce, and I know his family. They wouldn't have let it go. They would have traced him here. That's a chance I won't let Marcus take."

Hunter looked thoughtful for a minute, then leaned down and hugged her. "Thank you for that." He stood again. "But I understand what my brother is feeling right now. If that had been Emily, the motherfucker would be dead."

"Even if she asked you not to?" Roxy wanted to hear that she had done the right thing. She knew she had for herself, but she had no idea if she had done right by Marcus. *It's the shifters' way*, kept echoing in her head.

"That's a hard one, Roxy." Hunter sat down next to her and sighed. "That's a real hard one. Our ways are different from humans'. And there's nothing more sacred to us than our mates. It's the shifter way."

Hearing those words sent her heart to her stomach. She wanted to throw up. She needed to talk to Marcus. Now. "Where is he?" When Hunter just shook his head, she stood. "Please, Hunter. Where's Marcus? I know you know."

"Shit," Hunter grumbled, then stood. "Come on, but I want free coffee for life for taking you because I'm damn sure there will be an ass kicking in my future.

"You got it," Roxy promised, following him. Her need to see Marcus was so strong she would have promised him anything.

# Chapter 15

Marcus slammed his way out of the coffee shop and headed down the road. He passed people who were staring at him and the coffee shop. Questions were called out toward him, but he continued heading away. He needed to get the fuck away from there before he went back on his promise, a fucking promise that he hadn't wanted to make, and kill the son of a bitch.

Flashes of Roxy's ex standing over her with his fist raised and her cowering in the corner had his blood boiling to the point he almost turned around more than once. She had no idea what she had asked of him when she made him promise not to kill Bruce.

Hearing Dell shouting his name had him walking faster until he was in a full-out run. He was torn with so many emotions that his wolf raged inside him, but he refused his wolf freedom because he knew his wolf didn't have his control and would turn around and tear the motherfucker's throat out. Leaving Roxy was also the hardest thing he had ever done. She was hurt but proved she was strong enough to stand up to her ex-husband. He was pissed and proud all at the same time.

"Fuck!" Marcus shouted as he ran into the woods, not stopping until he was in a clearing. *His* clearing. He had visited this spot to think since they'd moved here. It wasn't far from town, but hard to find, and it was silent except for the sounds of the woods. It was his sanctuary, where he could lose his shit when needed and right now, he needed to lose his shit.

Marcus walked further into the clearing, his breathing hard and fast. Punching a tree as he passed didn't even faze him.

"Fuck!" he raged, scaring a few birds out of hiding. Her bruised face flashed through his mind again, and he punched out, smashing his hand into a different tree. Dropping to his knees, he threw his head back and howled his fury until he was out of breath.

Dropping his head forward, his eyes opened, staring at the dirt beneath his knees. His eyes blurred for a second, but he blinked repeatedly. He had failed her. He had failed to keep her safe, and the bastard who harmed her was within his grasp, yet he'd done nothing. His breathing calmed, his mind clearing as he stared at nothing, wondering where he went from there.

Hearing a noise, his head snapped up. His eyes spotted her immediately. She looked like an angel standing in his clearing. Then he looked closer and saw her face. He looked back down, squeezing his eyes shut as if that would clear the brutal reminder from his mind. He heard her coming closer but didn't look up. He couldn't do it.

"Hunter brought me." Her voice reached his ears, making his head tilt, but his eyes remained closed, his head still lowered. "I'm sorry, Marcus."

Slowly, his head rose, and his eyes opened. "You've nothing to be sorry for."

"I made you promise something that's against what you believe," Roxy whispered, then cleared her throat and squared her shoulders. "I know what I made you promise is not the 'shifter way.'"

"No, it's not." Marcus frowned, his eyes shifting away from her beautiful bruised face. "He should be dead by my hand."

She knelt in front of him, but far enough away to give him space. "But that's not my way." Roxy leaned closer, trying to get him to look at her. "His family would have traced him here, Marcus. And that's not a chance I want to take. I'm not worth—"

"Don't even say it." Marcus finished with a warning growl, his eyes shooting toward her. "You are worth it. It's my duty, my honor to protect my mate, and I failed."

"You didn't fail, Marcus." Roxy looked him straight in the eye. "It's because of you that I was able to stand up and take my life back. Do you know how humiliating it is to be beaten, see the pitying looks on people's faces? I'm a strong woman. Well, I was a strong woman before I met Bruce."

"There's nothing weak about you." Marcus frowned.

"There was. But because I want a life with you, I found my strength again. I took back the power that he stole from me. I want you to teach me how to protect myself. I want to get my concealed carry. I want to put a restraining order on him. I need to call the police in California to warn them about his threats against my parents. For the first time since the abuse started, I want to take action, and I'm not afraid to because I have you at my side." Roxy finally reached out to touch his hand. "If you kill him and get arrested—"

"I wouldn't get arrested. We have ways," Marcus responded, cutting her off.

"Okay, then we wouldn't have worked. Knowing you killed a man, even a bastard like Bruce because of me when there was another away, would haunt me." Roxy sighed, then smiled sadly. "I guess I wasn't made to be part of the shifters' way of life. I just know that I can't do or be the strong woman I want to be without you by my side. I can't do any of this without you. I want to make you proud, Marcus. I want to be proud of myself, and I haven't been for a very long time. I did what I had to do today because if not, you wouldn't get all of me."

Marcus stared at the woman kneeling in the dirt before him, and he had never loved anyone more. There would never be anyone in his lifetime that he loved as much as he loved Roxy Patel.

"I just wanted to tell you that and to tell you I'm sorry." Roxy started to stand, but he grasped the hand that rested on his, stopping her.

"I'm not going anywhere." His voice was rough with emotion. "And I've never been prouder of anyone in my life than I was of you."

"Then why did you leave?" Roxy tilted her head, uncertainty in her eyes.

"To keep my promise to you," Marcus replied, honestly. "You asked a lot of me when you asked me to promise not to kill him. I promised you not because of fear for me, but because of the love I have for you. Don't you know by now that I would do anything for you? I would kill for you. I would, obviously, *not* kill for you. I would lay down my life for you."

Roxy's head dropped, and her tears hit the dirt between them. As she started to look back up, she gasped. "What happened to your hand?"

He looked down to see his hand torn to hell, his blood smeared on hers. "I hit a tree... or two."

"We need to clean that," she said absently, then glanced at the tree. "Why did you do that?"

"Because I promised my mate I wouldn't kill a man." He pulled her to him. She willingly came to him and straddled his lap. "So I decided to kill a few trees."

"I love you, Marcus Foster," Roxy whispered, putting her forehead against his.

"And I love you, Roxy." Marcus kissed her, then quickly pulled away when she hissed in pain. Anger hit him hard, and once again he had to push it away. "I'm sorry."

"I'll heal." She hugged him tightly, then laid her head on his shoulder. "It's beautiful here."

"Yes, it is. I come here often when I want to be alone." Marcus frowned. "So how in the hell did Hunter know where I was?"

"I don't know, but I asked him to take me to you, and he did, so now I have to give him free coffee for life," she replied, then shivered, cuddling closer to him.

Marcus chuckled. "Yeah, that sounds like Hunter."

"It's snowing." Roxy lifted her head off his shoulder and tilted her head back to look at the sky through the trees.

Marcus watched the flakes floating around them, then noticed she didn't even have a coat on. "Where's your coat?"

"Don't need one with you holding me. You're so warm." Roxy snuggled closer. "I could stay here forever."

Her words hit home with him. He had thought that so many times sitting in this clearing. "Roxy."

She stopped peering at the sky and falling snow flurries to look at him. "Yes?"

"I'm not prepared, but there will never be a better time than this time right now." Marcus glanced down at the ground and grabbed a twig and quickly broke it at length, knotted the two ends together, and looked back at her. "Will you marry me?"

Before she could even comprehend what he asked, Marcus felt maybe it wasn't the time and second-guessed his impulse to ask.

"I mean, I know you're probably not ready, and this isn't the ideal place for a proposal." He looked down at the oddly made ring in his hand. "And this isn't really the ring that I would—"

"Shut up." Roxy's voice cracked.

"I'll understand—"

"Shut up, Marcus." Roxy put both hands on each side of his face. "A million times yes. I will marry you."

"Really?" Marcus's eyes widened.

"This is the perfect place, perfect time..." She looked down at the twig ring in his hand, then lifted her left hand. "...and perfect ring."

He slipped it on her finger with a grin. "I promise to get you a better ring."

"This is the ring that means something to me." Roxy looked down at it with a smile. "I'll cherish it."

"I cherish you." Marcus kissed the side of her mouth that wasn't split. "I will always cherish you."

\*\*\*\*\*\*

As Marcus carried her out of the woods, she was in absolute heaven. "I can walk, Marcus." She sighed, not really wanting him to put her down. But they had been walking for a while, which made her lift her head from his shoulder and look around. "Where are we? My house wasn't that far away."

"No way am I putting you down." Marcus smiled down at her. "And we aren't going to your house. We are going to our home."

They emerged from the woods, and before them was a two-story log cabin with a wraparound porch and a red tin roof. "Please tell me that is real?" Roxy straightened in his arms, her eyes taking everything in.

"It's absolutely real," Marcus said proudly. "And it's all yours."

"Ours," Roxy said absently, then wriggled to get set down. Once her feet hit the ground, she ran up to the porch and laughed. "I've always wanted a log cabin with a wraparound porch and tin roof."

"I know." Marcus walked toward her and leaned against the railing. "I heard you talking to Clare one day."

Her heart fluttered at his words. She remembered that day. She had just opened the coffee shop, and Marcus had been their first customer. He sat at one of the tables while she and Clare excitedly talked about their plans for the shop. She also said her goal was to one day have a log cabin in the woods with a wraparound porch and a red tin roof. Suddenly, everything was too much, and the tears along with the racking sobs from her soul started.

"Roxy?" Marcus sounded concerned as he jumped over the railing and pulled her into his arms. "What is it? I'll change whatever you don't like."

His words made her cry harder and then laugh. She was laughing and crying all over him. "It's perfect." She hiccupped. "It's just so much. No one has ever done anything like this for me. You heard something I said and made it come true. Who does that?"

"The man who loves you," Marcus answered without hesitation. "And I would tear it down and start again if you were displeased."

"I don't deserve you." Roxy cried, then laughed again. "And I really have to stop crying because it's really hurting my face."

"You deserve everything," Marcus said, then frowned. "Come on, let's go inside and tend to our wounds."

Roxy followed him, her swollen red eyes taking in everything and already making plans on where her garden would go, where the two rocking chairs would sit on the porch, and then she walked through the open doorway Marcus had unlocked. "Oh my God!" she whispered in awe.

"I didn't furnish anything because I want it all to be your touch." Marcus walked further into the room. "Check it out while I start a fire and get the first-aid kit I have stashed."

At a loss for words, Roxy nodded, looking around like a kid in a toy store for the first time. She was amazed and dazed all at once. Seeing the staircase, she ran up it. There were two bedrooms and a small loft room, which she fell in love with.

"Well, what do you think?" Marcus had come up the stairs, his eyes on her.

"It's a dream." Roxy hugged him tightly. "I love it doesn't even describe my feelings."

Marcus smiled proudly. "Every piece of wood, nail, and anything else was done with you in mind."

"Thank you!" She kissed him, but when their lips hit, she hissed in pain. "Dammit. I want to kiss you so bad."

"Come on." He took her hand and led her back downstairs. He already had a fire burning in the fireplace with blankets and pillows in front of it.

She kicked off her shoes before she sat down on the blankets and waited while he threw another log on the fire. It was growing dark, but the glow from the fire provided just enough light. He sat in front of her and reached for the first-aid kit. He had a bowl of water and towels. He wet a towel then gently started wiping the dried blood from her face. The more he stared at her face, the more his eyes darkened with anger. She knew the sight of her battered face was sending him over the edge, but she wanted him here, present, without the anger toward her ex.

"I can do this, Marcus." Roxy didn't want to spoil the mood.

"Am I hurting you?" He stopped, waiting for her answer.

"No, not at all." She would have lied if he were hurting her, because she knew he needed to do this. His next words proved that.

"So, is this promise I made you a lifetime promise?" Marcus studied her lip, his eyes not rising to meet hers.

"Are you asking me if there are holes in the promise you made me?" She tilted her head so she could see better in the firelight.

"Yes, I am." He dipped the towel in the water and wrung it out.

Tension flickered between them, and he stopped his hand from rising to her face when she said, "If he comes back, he's coming back to kill me." Roxy knew her words were true. "But I don't think that will happen because he's a coward, and I saw fear in his eyes. Fear of you. I've never seen him afraid of anything. So because I know he'll never come back, then no, it's not a lifetime promise."

"Good, because if he steps foot within twenty miles of you and I know about it, he's a dead man." Marcus continued to clean her face.

Her stomach dipped at his protectiveness, something she had never really felt from a man before. Soon, it was her turn to clean his wound on his hand. "I can't believe you punched a tree."

"Yeah, well, I needed to hit something," Marcus grumbled, then hissed when she patted the open cuts with peroxide.

"Don't be a baby," she teased, then dabbed some more.

"Hey, that shit stings." Marcus's frown turned into a grin when Roxy started blowing on it.

"Can we stay here tonight?" she asked, then watched his smile grow. God, she loved his smile. It felt like home, and how dumb did that sound? But it was so true.

"Absolutely." He grabbed the bloody towel, water, and peroxide, putting it out of the way.

Settling down, they talked, laughed, and just enjoyed each other's company. Soon they lay together, quietly watching the fire, with her in front of him, cuddled tightly against him. As she stared at the flames, Roxy savored the peace that settled over her.

"Thank you," she whispered.

"For what?" he asked against her ear.

"Loving me."

"You're my life." Marcus held her tighter. "And I'm never letting go."

# Chapter 16

Marcus stood in Jonah's kitchen looking at Ross and the six men who were ready to join their pack. There had been no more signs or messages from her stepbrother, Carl, in the last week. Though Ross made it clear that she'd believed it when Carl had said he wasn't done. Since she knew him best, the pack listened to her and were instructed to not let their guard down.

"Any problems last night?" Marcus asked Dell who had been on training duty with them. It was essential that they knew the layout of the land. They'd already run the route and learned it in their human form. Now they were running it in their wolf form.

"No," Dell responded with his usual one-word response.

"Ah, okay." Marcus looked at each of them. "Anyone having a hard time with remembering their route?"

"No," again was Dell's answer.

"Well, okay." Marcus grinned. "Always good talking to you, Dell."

Leda walked in, then stopped quickly. Marcus noticed her eyes stopped on Devon, one of the new shifters, and looked away quickly, her face turning pink.

"Garrett's looking for you," she said quickly.

Marcus glanced at Devon, then back to Leda with a raised eyebrow. "Okay, well, I'm here where he told me to be."

"Hey, I'm just delivering the message," Leda shot back with narrowed eyes, then turned to leave. "I'll tell him you said he's an idiot for not knowing you were where he told you to be."

The guys laughed, even Ross chuckled. "Smartass."

"You taught me well, Marcus," Leda shot back before hurrying out the door.

"Okay, take the rest of the day off," Marcus instructed the group. "Get some rest because I'll be testing you over the next night or two." Marcus headed out, catching up with Leda. "So, what was that?"

"What was what?" Leda frowned, picking up her pace.

"Your googly eyes at Devon. I thought you had something going with Steve, the mighty vampire warrior." Marcus loved teasing Leda. She was quick-witted and always had funny comebacks.

"Ain't no ring on this finger." Leda flipped her hand up in the air. "And what the hell are googly eyes?"

"There better not be a ring on any of those fingers. You're too young, and Garrett has two babies on the way so he can't afford to be killing some kid because he was stupid enough to give you a ring. And googly eyes, you know, what you were doing with Devon." Marcus batted his eyelashes, mocking her.

Leda glared at him. "Steve is busy and so am I. We hardly talk. And I did not do that thing you just did with your eyeballs to Devon."

"Good because he's too old for you," Marcus warned. She was like his kid sister, and there would be hell to pay if some horny-ass guy sniffed around her.

"No, he's not," Leda grouched as she veered off and headed toward the coffee shop. "I swear I'm never going to be able to date normally."

"Probably not," Marcus called after her as he opened the door to Garrett's and walked in, then wished he hadn't. Sadie sat in the kitchen crying while Garrett looked like he wanted to kill somebody.

"Where's Roxy?" Garrett frowned, looking behind Marcus. "I told Leda to get you both."

"The coffee shop." Marcus glanced at Sadie who openly stared at him as she dabbed at her eyes, which were tearless at the moment. One side of her mouth was still puffy from Roxy's fist. "And it's probably best she stays there."

"I wanted to apologize." Sadie sniffed, but Marcus wasn't falling for it. "I really didn't realize how bad it was between Roxy and Bruce."

Leda and Roxy walked in talking and smiling until they saw Sadie sitting with Garrett and Marcus.

Marcus pulled her to him, giving her a kiss on the cheek. "Keep calm, killer," he whispered with a grin.

"I'm calm," Roxy said, loud enough for everyone to hear. Her eyes stayed on Sadie. "For now."

"Roxy, I'm really sorry about what happened," Sadie said, then looked down at her hands. "I met your ex in Lexington when I was there on business."

Marcus knew she was lying and wanted to call her out on it early so they could get past the bullshit, but Roxy beat him to it.

"Sadie, that's too much of a coincidence." Roxy shook her head. "I don't believe you. How did you get the information on my ex?"

"That's not a lie." Sadie struggled to keep calm, they all could see it. "I met him in Lexington."

"Sadie, I lived with a lying, manipulative man for longer than I'd like to admit. And you don't hold a candle to him when it comes to either of those things." Roxy frowned, anger filtering through the calm façade she was trying to maintain. "So why don't you just tell the truth for once in your life and come clean. If not, I'm busy and need to get back to it."

"He wants me to move. To leave town." Sadie pointed at Marcus and started crying again, obviously wanting to deflect from answering Roxy. "I don't have anywhere else to go. I've lived here all my life. I've apologized, and I'm not lying. I didn't realize how bad it was between you and your ex."

"You put my mate in danger." Marcus growled the words, not falling for her lies, making Sadie cry harder. He glanced at Garrett and rolled his eyes.

"Honestly, this is a waste of time." Roxy sighed. "I really don't care what she does or doesn't do as long as she stays away from me. What's done is done."

"It's your call, Roxy," Garrett said, his arms crossed, looking as if he would rather be anywhere but there dealing with this shit.

"I thought I just made it. I don't care." Roxy glanced down at Sadie. "But fair warning, Sadie. Stay away from me and mine."

"Why is everyone so mad at me. I didn't do anything." Sadie's voice rose slightly, but she was still doing the "feel sorry for me" act that no one was buying.

"You did plenty and got caught," Roxy replied, then kissed Marcus on the cheek. "I have to get back to the coffee shop. Do whatever, but I'm not making that decision. She's been warned to stay away from me."

Marcus watched Roxy walk out before turning toward Garrett. "Now what?"

"Go home, Sadie." Garrett sighed, rubbing his forehead.

"Am I allowed to keep my home?" she asked, looking between Garrett and Marcus.

"For now," Garrett replied, dropping his hand. "But you start trouble with anyone else in my pack, you will be asked to leave, is that understood?"

"Yes." Sadie stood from the chair, then headed toward the door. "Thank you."

Marcus watched her leave and knew this wasn't the end. "That sounded real sincere." He curled his lip.

"I can't just kick her out of her home, Marcus. She's not a shifter, so my authority over her is not like it is over our pack." Garrett cursed and headed toward the kitchen. "So stop making threats to people until you talk to me first, dammit. It puts me in a bad spot."

"She's trouble and has been trouble." Marcus knew when he'd demanded that Sadie left in his fit of rage he was overstepping his bounds, but it was the only thing he could think to say to her when everything went down that fit his anger.

"Like I don't know that." Garrett sat down heavily on one of the stools.

"You okay?" Marcus noticed how tired his brother looked.

"Haven't been getting much sleep." Garrett rubbed his forehead again. "Janna's having a hard time again."

"Damn, man." Marcus sat across from him. "Anything I can do?"

"Yeah, stop making threats that we can't act on." Garrett glared at him.

"She isn't finished. You know that, right?"

"Yes, I know that." Garrett glanced toward the hallway, cocking his head. "And we need to keep a close eye on her. Janna's up. I need to get up there."

"Have you called Slade?" Marcus stood, wishing there was more he could do to help Garrett and Janna.

"Yeah, been talking to him daily." Garrett grabbed some orange juice out of the fridge, then headed toward the hallway. "He's going to be making a trip to see her in the next couple of days."

That was good, Marcus thought. He needed to speak to the doc himself. He and Roxy had never used protection. With his makeup, he didn't get the diseases that humans got and he couldn't pass anything to her either, so in that they were safe. He could get her pregnant, but she was human. He had a lot of questions about that. Their mother had been human also, and they'd turned out fine, well, all except Hunter. That thought made him chuckle. Thoughts of having a family with Roxy made him smile. With a glance at his watch, he stood and headed out of Garrett's. In just a few hours, he and Roxy could begin working on that family.

# Chapter 17

"You okay?" Clare asked as soon as Roxy walked back in.

"Yeah." Roxy sighed, trying to keep her anger in check. She just wanted to be happy and lose the anger. "Sadie was at Garrett's asking for forgiveness."

"Oh, I bet that was a sight." Clare snorted. "Were there tears involved?"

"Oh yeah." Roxy rolled her eyes. "And sniffing."

"Fake as her tits, I'm sure." Clare snickered.

"She got a boob job?" Roxy's interest was piqued.

"Ain't no way those puppies are real." Clare poured herself some coffee and leaned against the counter. "She left town for about two weeks a few years ago and came back with a new bra size."

"Why is she so...?"

"Much of a bitch? A ho?" Clare shrugged a shoulder. "She's been that way since we were in school. Always going after other girls' boyfriends, two-faced, and the only friend she's ever really had was Deb. She uses her so bad, but Deb doesn't see it."

"I really would like to know how she found my ex's information to get in contact with him." Roxy frowned. "I know I've never really talked about it with anyone except you and I know you'd never tell anyone anything, especially her."

"Damn straight." Clare finished off her coffee. "I'm the best bestie you'll ever have. Now, let's stop talking about hos and tell me when your furniture's coming in."

Roxy grinned in total agreement. She was done talking about Sadie Johnson. The day after Marcus had shown her the house, he had taken her into Lexington to pick out furniture. It was a totally different experience than when she furnished the house she'd lived in with Bruce. Everything she had picked out with her ex he disagreed with, so in truth, everything in the house was his touch, not hers. With Marcus, he'd just stood back watching her decide what she liked and then told the sales person to order it. At first, she had been uncomfortable, looking at price tags and passing things up she felt were too expensive. Marcus had figured out what she was doing and took his phone out, pulled up his bank account and showed her, saying that was the money they had, so spend what she wanted. After that, she felt a little better, but still watched and calculated in her head as they went along.

"Most of it comes in today after two," Roxy said, her excitement filling her voice. "Marcus is coming to get me."

"He's a good guy." Clare nodded. "And has been in love with you since the day you came to town."

Before Roxy could agree, the door opened and in walked Dell with the new shifters. Roslyn was with them.

"Hello, ladies." Dell smiled, walking toward them with the crew following.

"Hi," Clare said, her cheeks blushing as she looked shyly away from Dell.

Roxy did a double take at Clare. Dell? Well, how in the hell hadn't she seen that? She quickly turned her attention back to Dell. "Hey, you all wanting some coffee? I also baked some cupcakes."

"Cupcakes?" One of the men behind Dell peeked around with interest. "I'd love a cupcake."

Clare disappeared in the back, then reappeared with a platter of freshly baked cupcakes and set them on the counter. "Best cupcakes in Kentucky." She smiled. "Have at it."

Clare and Roxy filled coffee and drinks for them as Dell sat quietly at the counter as the others talked. She watched as Clare filled his cup without saying a word. Clare, quiet... yeah, something was going on there. Roxy followed Clare to the back.

"We're running low on sugar out front." Clare reached up, getting some. "I'll refill them before we close, but everything else should be stocked."

"Sounds good." Roxy rinsed out a pot, but she watched Clare. "Dell sure is good-looking."

Clare was reaching up for another box of sugar packets just as Roxy spoke and dropped it on her face. "Ouch." She rubbed her forehead. "Dammit, Roxy."

"You okay?" Roxy asked, trying to sound concerned, but her laughter blew that.

Clare bent down to grab the box. "Yes."

"Yes, you're okay, or yes, Dell is a fine-looking man?" Roxy raised an eyebrow.

Clare thought for a moment, then glanced toward the door that led to the front of the shop. "Yes, on both counts." She balanced the boxes, then just stood there. "But he doesn't know I exist."

"Oh, I don't know about that." Roxy kinda wished she had kept her mouth shut seeing the disappointment on Clare's face.

"Well, I do. What would a man like that want with me, anyway?" Clare shrugged, almost losing the boxes but regained control. "It's all good. I get to look, and I likey what I see."

Feeling bad for bringing it up, Roxy dried her hands and headed back out front. Dell was taking the boxes from her and taking them where she needed them. Thoughts of matchmaking filled her mind, but she paused when she saw Roslyn—she just couldn't get used to calling the beautiful girl Ross—watching Dell out of the corner of her eye. Okay, maybe she better leave well enough alone and let whatever happened, happen. Her eyes moved over the rest of the shifters. She had to admit, shifters were a good-looking lot. Big, strong, and good hair—what the hell was that all about anyway? The men had better hair than her. When she first came to town, Marcus had kept his short, in a military cut, but was now wearing it longer. She loved his hair either way, but his longer hair made him look wilder, and she really liked that.

"The real reason we came over here was so I could introduce you to these guys, not eat everything you had to offer and drink all your coffee." Dell smiled as he turned toward them. "Garrett wants all the businesses to know them, and them know you. First, what do I owe you for all this?"

"Put your wallet away." Roxy frowned at him. "The cupcakes were on the house. I made them because we were slow and I was bored. I also wanted to try a new recipe, so you guys were my guinea pigs, so to speak. Hope you don't get sick later."

Seeing concern on a few faces, she laughed.

"Just kidding," Roxy continued. "And we are getting ready to close so the coffee would have been poured out anyway."

Dell nodded but didn't put his wallet away. "I think you've both met Ross." Dell nodded her way.

"We have." Roxy smiled at the blonde as did Clare.

"This is James, Les, Devon, Taz, and Josh." Dell pointed them out.

"Nice to meet you." The one named Devon smiled.

Roxy nodded, knowing right off the bat that one was a charmer. He was handsome with blue eyes, which she had never seen with any of the shifters she'd ever met. "It's nice meeting you all."

"Devon and Taz are both going to be in charge of your business as well as seeing you home safely until things are back under control." Dell turned back to Roxy, then glanced at Clare. "Do not leave to go home without one of them knowing. If you walk, they will walk with you. If you drive, they will make sure you get to your car okay."

"No prob." Clare nodded in understanding.

Dell turned his attention back to Roxy. "Marcus approved them." He gave her a grin.

"Oh, is that a thing? Marcus approved." Roxy laughed, shaking her head.

"It is now." Dell pulled out a fifty from his wallet and placed it on the counter. "Don't argue because I won't take it back."

Roxy started to open her mouth, but he was already heading for the door. "Thanks, and it was nice meeting you guys."

"Don't fuck up," Dell warned both Devon and Taz on his way out.

"Doesn't hesitate to say what he means, huh?" Roxy's eyebrows rose, and she smiled at them.

"Tell us about it." Devon stood and headed toward Clare. "You need help with anything?"

"Well, if you're offering, the garbage needs to be taken out." Clare grinned and headed toward the back. "I won't pass up help with that job."

Roxy laughed and looked toward Taz who sat quietly. His eyes were intense as he looked around. "You need anything, Taz?" Roxy asked, wanting to make him feel comfortable. He was a good-looking guy with long black hair and high cheekbones. She wondered if he was part Native American.

"No, ma'am." His voice was deeper than she expected for someone his age. He couldn't be more than nineteen or twenty, but he carried himself as someone much older.

"Are you from around here?" She made small talk as she prepared to close up for the night.

"Yes." His one-word answer indicated to her that he wasn't much for small talk.

The door opened and in rushed Leda. "Hey! Marcus wanted me to tell you that he would be here in a few minutes and not to leave." Leda frowned. "I think I'm going to start charging them a fee for each message I deliver. Seriously, what do they think I am? A personal messaging service? Haven't they heard of text messaging?"

Roxy watched Taz, who was staring at Leda. A small smile appeared on his lips at her words but quickly disappeared when Devon appeared with Clare. Then they narrowed and looked away. Interesting.

"Hey, Devon." Leda smiled shyly.

"Well, hello, cutie." Devon gave her that charming smile. "What are you doing here?"

"Giving Roxy a message from Marcus," Leda replied, then looked toward Taz, obviously noticing him for the first time. "Oh, hi, Taz. I'm sorry, I didn't see you sitting there."

Taz gave her a nod without looking directly at her. Just as things were getting interesting, Marcus came in the door. "You just now gave her the message?" He frowned at Leda. "What the hell have you been doing? I told you half an hour ago."

"Don't start on me, Marcus." Leda glared at him. "I had two other messages to deliver when I got yours, and honestly, Garrett scares me more than you do."

"I can change that real quick." Marcus glared back at her.

Leda snorted. "Sure, whatever. I know we live in the middle of nowhere, but there is a thing called texting. I'm going to start charging for these messages so get your wallet ready."

With that, she headed out the door without waiting to hear Marcus's reply. Roxy noticed two things at once. Devon watched Leda go with a leering look she wasn't comfortable with. Taz was watching Devon with a deadly look of fury on his face.

"You ready?" Marcus was in front of her, his eyes searching hers. "Something wrong?"

"I don't know." She frowned, then shook her head at his look. "I'll tell you later. Let me finish up real quick."

As she headed toward the back, she glanced at Devon who Clare was talking to, but Devon was staring at Roxy, his eyes roaming up and down her body. When he noticed Roxy looking at him, he gave her a wink then turned his attention back to Clare. She looked over her shoulder to see Marcus talking to Taz, missing the exchange.

Once in the back, she checked the back door to make sure it was locked, then turned off the lights. Clare peeked her head in. "You got it?"

Roxy grabbed her arm and pulled Clare into the darkness. "Don't trust, Devon," she whispered, her eyes on the door to make sure they were alone.

"What? Why?" Clare whispered back. "He's hot."

"I'm serious, Clare. There's something about him." Roxy saw that she wasn't taking her seriously. "Trust me on this. Don't trust him. Living the hell I lived, I pay special attention, especially where men are concerned, and something is not right. He might just be a player, but even that should make you realize, hot or not, he's not worth the trouble."

"Damn," Clare cursed, but nodded. "Okay, I trust you."

"Good." Roxy started to head out of the back, but Clare stopped her.

"Not even a little tickle—"

"No," Roxy said with as much seriousness as she could, but then noticed Clare gave her a teasing grin. "Not even to tickle his pickle, you ho."

"I love you, man." Clare gave her a big sideways hug as they walked out.

"You better, or I'll tell Sadie you need a new bestie," Roxy warned, then laughed when they both tried to fit through the door side by side.

"Bitch." Clare pushed through first.

"Ho," Roxy shot back.

All three men were watching them. Marcus laughed. "Did you just call my mate a bitch?"

"She called me a ho," Clare defended herself.

"I'll walk you home," Devon said to Clare out of the blue.

Roxy and Clare shared a look. "No, that's okay, but thank you," Clare said, pulling out car keys and dangling them. "I drove today."

As if Marcus sensed something going on, he stepped in. "Why don't you and Taz head on back to Jonah's and see if Dell has something else going on?" He opened the door for Roxy and Clare. "I'll make sure she gets to her car."

Taz walked out and headed down the street without saying a word and without Devon. Marcus took the keys and locked up, watching Devon, who looked pissed off.

"Okay, what was that all about?" Marcus took Roxy's hand as they walked Clare to her car.

"Ask her." Clare hit the button unlocking her car. "All I know is I'm not allowed to tickle his pickle."

Roxy laughed as Clare gave her a wave and got into her car. They watched as Clare drove away.

"Tickle his fucking pickle?" Marcus glared at her. "What in the hell do you two talk about?"

"You don't even want to know." Roxy leaned up and kissed him on the cheek. "I just don't trust Devon. He seems shifty and definitely a player."

They crossed the road, passed Garrett's house, and cut through the woods. "And you know this how?" Marcus squeezed her hand. "If that motherfucker made a pass at you—"

"He didn't," she replied, and it wasn't a lie. Looking inappropriately at her while flirting with her friend and even Leda wasn't making a pass at her. It was just a male player being an asshole. "But trust me on this one. Also, he has his eye on Leda, and I know Leda is—"

"Yeah, I know." Marcus frowned. "I saw her making googly eyes at him."

"What?" Roxy actually stopped to look at him.

"You know, googly eyes." He batted his eyelashes at her. "Googly eyes."

"First, promise me to never do whatever in the hell that was you did with your eyes again." Roxy shook her head. "And googly eyes is just... weird."

"Isn't that what it's called?" Marcus asked as they started walking again.

"No, thank God." Roxy glanced at him from the corner of her eye and knew he was teasing. "Googly eyes." She laughed, shaking her head again. God, she loved this man.

# Chapter 18

"Roxy, this is not up for discussion." Marcus growled as he stood behind her while she was on the ladder hanging a picture. "I have to head into town, and you're not staying here alone."

"I'll be fine, Marcus." Roxy leaned back on the ladder to look at the picture. "How does that look?"

Marcus wasn't looking at the picture, but her ass as she stood above him. "Nice." He grinned. "Real fucking nice."

Roxy looked over her shoulder at him and sighed. "The picture, Marcus."

"Yeah, it looks good." Marcus winked at her without even looking at the picture.

It had been a week since all the furniture had been delivered and they had spent all their free time making their new house a home as well as planning a wedding. He was in absolute love with his mate and couldn't get enough of her. Would never get enough of her.

"Catch me," Roxy said before letting go of the ladder.

"Dammit, stop doing that." Marcus caught her easily enough, but it still made him nervous when she did shit like that. What if he wasn't paying attention? Yeah, like that would happen, he thought to himself.

"I like when you catch me." Roxy grinned, placing a finger in the cleft of his chin. "I trust you."

"You still aren't staying here alone." Marcus cocked his eyebrow at her, knowing exactly what her game was, but enjoying the way she was playing it. A flirting Roxy usually ended up being a naked Roxy. She was beautiful, and he was relieved that her face was healing. It was so hard to keep his promise day after day seeing the damage the bastard had done to her.

"Who are you having come here?" Roxy sighed with a roll of her eyes.

"Not sure, I think everyone is busy at the moment, as I should be." Marcus glanced at his phone. "You're going to get me in trouble with my alpha. Maybe Dell can come over."

"This is ridiculous." Roxy huffed. "You have this place set up like Fort Knox. No one is getting in here. I'll be fine."

"No."

"But—"

"No."

"You're so frustrating," Roxy grumbled. "Hey, how about Roslyn."

"Ross?" Marcus glanced up from his phone. "No."

"Her name is Roslyn, and why not?" Roxy had turned and was looking at the newly hung picture, turning her head this way and that. "She knows her stepbrother more than anyone. I'd feel safer with her because of that fact. Plus, there hasn't been any sign of him, right? So maybe he got bored and took off."

Marcus grinned, but it was quickly replaced with a frown. There was no way Carl had taken off. Wolf shifters didn't like to have their asses kicked, and they certainly had the tendency for revenge. From what

Ross had told them, he was crazy, so Marcus wasn't taking any chances.

"No," Marcus repeated, then looked up to see her trying to move the heavy ladder. Gently, he moved her out of the way. "Where do you want it?"

"Over there." She pointed to the wall near the window. "Don't you trust Roslyn?"

"Not completely, no." Marcus looked up and judged the distance before placing the ladder down. He then turned to see her confusion. "Roxy, honestly, I only trust myself with your safety as well as my brothers and Dell. I don't know these new shifters enough to trust them with you."

"Oh." Roxy bit her lip, staring at him. "I'm sorry I'm being difficult. It's just with work and with what you have to do, we don't have a lot of time."

He walked toward her and took her in his arms. "And I told you that you could quit the coffee shop anytime you wanted."

"I don't want to quit." She hesitated before answering, which pissed him off because he knew the reason why. Her ex had made sure she had no means to support herself. It was a fear that she was battling, and he understood it had nothing to do with him personally, but it still pissed him the fuck off.

"And that's fine." Marcus groaned when his phone rang. Grabbing it, he looked at the screen and cursed. "I really need to go."

"Okay, let me get my coat." Roxy sighed, then pulled away.

Marcus watched her go and wished it was different, but until he felt it was safe for her to be here alone, he wasn't budging on his decisions. Her safety was his top priority.

"I'm ready." She gave him a small smile.

"It shouldn't take long," Marcus said as he locked up. "We'll take the car."

"Good because it's cold." Roxy snuggled in her coat as she headed for the car.

They drove into town and pulled into Garrett's. "It'll get better," Marcus said as he shut off the engine. "I promise."

"I know it will." Roxy leaned over and kissed him. "I'm sorry for being a pain in your ass and making you late."

Marcus chuckled as he climbed out and hurried to open her door. "I'm always late, and you'll make it up to me tonight."

"Good to know." Roxy wrapped her arm around him. "I'll make sure to be a bigger pain in the ass on a daily basis."

"Now, wait a minute." Marcus laughed, squeezing her tightly as they climbed the steps. "A bigger pain in the ass, I don't know about that. You're too sweet to be a bigger pain in the ass."

"You have no clue." Roxy walked inside with a grin. "I'm putting on my best behavior act until you're mine officially."

Before they could reach the kitchen, where they heard everyone, Marcus pulled her back into him, wrapping his arms around her stomach. "I already am yours, official or not, so no worries there." He bit her neck. "Give me your worst, and it wouldn't make a damn bit of difference."

With that said, he walked her into the kitchen still in his arms, both of them wearing huge smiles. Emily, Janna, Garrett, and Hunter all stood around talking.

"Get a damn room," Hunter said as they appeared.

"How you feeling?" Roxy smiled at Janna.

"Fat." Janna shifted on the stool.

"You're beautiful." Marcus kissed her on the cheek then dodged Garrett's punch.

"Roxy, keep your man off my woman, would you, before I kick his ass?" Garrett growled with a grin.

"Okay, what's the plan?" Marcus was ready to get whatever he had to do done so he could get back home with Roxy. *Home.* Damn, that sounded right.

"Head on over to Jonah's." Garrett became instantly serious. "Taz picked up Carl's scent, and he's not alone. He said there were five different scents. He's one hell of a tracker and a big asset to our pack. I want him to lead you, Hunter, Dell, and the rest of the new guys to where he picked up the scent. I'm staying here. Slade is on his way and should be here anytime to check up on Janna."

"If you need to go, I'll be fine," Janna said, rubbing her growing stomach.

"No," Garrett responded with a shake of his head. "They can handle it. Just keep me updated."

"No problem." Marcus leaned down and kissed Roxy. "Stay here and don't leave."

"Yes, sir." Roxy grinned when he narrowed his eyes.

He seemed to think for a minute then gave her a thoughtful look. "I kind of like that sir stuff."

Roxy rolled her eyes. "Don't get used to it."

He gave her a wink before walking out the door with Hunter.

\*\*\*\*\*\*

Roxy sat in the kitchen, glad that she was there. She was enjoying talking to Janna and Emily, making plans for the babies.

"How's the house coming along?" Emily asked, taking a bite of apple pie she had brought over.

"Great. I've never had so much fun and actually gave Marcus crap about leaving today." She laughed. "It's just between my work and what he does, we have very limited free time."

"I know what you mean." Emily sighed. "I never realized what it took to rebuild a business, and Deb is no help."

"Speaking of Deb." Janna glanced at Roxy. "Thank you for what you did. I heard what happened and if I wasn't so pregnant, I would have kicked her ass."

"It was my pleasure, believe me." Roxy snorted, relieved that Janna wasn't too upset about her punching one of her guests at the baby shower. "Sorry, Emily. I know she's your sister."

"Yeah, well I punched her the next time I saw her, so no apology needed." Emily glanced at them both. "Terrible isn't it, but God, it felt good."

They all started laughing just as Garrett walked in. He stopped, looking down at himself. "What?"

"We aren't laughing at you," Janna assured him. "We're laughing at Emily and Roxy's boxing skills."

The front door slammed, causing them all to turn that way. A man with a shotgun walked into the kitchen. Roxy stared in horror as he pointed at each of them. Everything happened so fast, no one had time to say anything or react. She watched in horror as Garrett didn't hesitate and rushed the man. She knew before it even happened that the man was going to pull the trigger. She screamed, but it was too late. The shotgun went off, and Garrett hit the floor. She tried to catch him, but he was too heavy. He fell halfway on her, but she was too busy staring at the man with the gun.

"What did you do?" she screamed as Janna dropped to the ground next to Garrett.

"No!" Janna screamed, trying to turn Garrett, his weight too much for her.

Roxy pulled her legs out from under Garrett and looked up to see another man grab Emily. Not really knowing what to do, she screamed at the top of her lungs, praying someone heard her. Her scream was cut short when something hard hit her in the head, and then all went black.

# Chapter 19

Marcus jogged to Jonah's, which was just down the road from Garrett's. Actually, everything was just down the road from Garrett's place which sat in the middle of town.

"What the fuck is the hurry?" Hunter jogged up next to him.

"I want to get back to my mate," Marcus said as he reached for the door. "Don't you?"

"Shut up, asshole." Hunter pushed him out of the way, going inside first. They both walked into the kitchen and stopped.

"Don't make a fucking move or I'll put a bullet in the back of his head." A man stood holding a gun to Jonah's head, who sat at the kitchen table.

Marcus did a quick sweep with his eyes and saw that every single one of them had walked into a fucking trap. "Who are you?"

"What gave you the impression that you could ask questions?" the man spat, his eyes shifting around seemingly monitoring everyone's moves.

Marcus made eye contact with Dell, who was the closest to the man, but he remained still, not wanting to spook him. "Guess I'm just the curious type."

"Get in here and sit against that wall. Don't make any moves or he's dead," the man ordered, pushing the gun into Jonah's head, making sure they got the message.

"I told these stupid fucks to go ahead and take him out." Jonah growled in disapproval, his eyes burning with anger. "I'm fucking old and don't give a shit if I die. Take him out!"

"Shut the fuck up." The man smacked Jonah on the side of the head, still holding the gun on him.

Both Marcus and Hunter slid down the wall, while Marcus's mind raced for a way out of this clusterfuck of a mess.

"You know...." Hunter started, and Marcus gave him a sideways glare.

"Man, don't piss the guy off." Marcus didn't know where Hunter was going with this, but Hunter always had a way out of situations, so he was going along with it hoping it didn't get Jonah killed.

"You know me. I piss everyone off." Hunter offered him a raised eyebrow.

"Both of you shut up," the man hissed, getting antsy, shifting from foot to foot.

"You know," Hunter restarted, ignoring the man's demand to shut up. "It's pretty badass that you have the Lee County wolves all under your control. I mean, that's some legendary shit right there. We're pretty well known as badasses ourselves."

Marcus watched the man closely and noticed he kept looking toward the door as if waiting for something or someone. This man was definitely a shifter, his wolf sensed it. He knew he couldn't send any messages mentally as they'd done before because most shifters could pick up on it. Instead, he glanced at Dell and eyed Jonah, then eyed the table. He did that three times and when Dell gave a short nod, he knew Dell understood. At least, he hoped he did.

"Is that why you're a little nervous?" Hunter asked. Not waiting for him to answer, he continued, "Because that's totally understandable. I'd also be nervous among legends. Hell, man, you'll probably be a hero, get all kinds of pussy. Shit, I want to be you, man."

"Will you just shut the fuck up?" the guy roared, his eyes going back to the door, his shifting from foot to foot going faster. He was sweating like a pig. He also didn't realize the faster he shifted his feet, the gun moved.

"Hey, just trying to break the tension." Hunter slowly scooted closer to the table, as did Marcus. Each time he looked at the door, they moved an inch. "So how much is Carl paying you? Hope you got your money up front, 'cause I heard he's broke as fuck and stiffed the last dumbass or, ah, guy who did a job for him."

"Shut the fuck up!" he screamed as he pointed the gun toward Hunter.

This was it. But before they could make their move, a loud gunshot echoed from outside. Everything happened at once. Dell went for Jonah as Marcus and Hunter both leaned back, kicked their feet up under the table and launched it at the man with everything they had. The gun clattered to the ground along with the table and the man, who was knocked out cold.

Marcus scrambled toward the man, making sure he was out, grabbed the gun and took off. "Make sure that fucker's tied up tight."

He followed Hunter out of the house, looking to see where the gunshot came from. People were out looking toward Garrett's. He saw Clare hurrying that way. "They said it came from Garrett's," she called out as they passed her.

Fear overtook any common sense Marcus had. He charged straight through the closed door; it splintered everywhere. His eyes searched for danger, searched for Roxy, and his heart stopped when he saw his brother lying in a puddle of blood, facedown on the floor.

"Goddammit!" He ran to Garrett, slipping in blood. With Hunter's help, they turned him over carefully. Marcus tore off his shirt while quickly examining the room, making sure Roxy wasn't lying on the floor somewhere, but she was gone, and so were Emily and Janna.

"Garrett!" Hunter shouted as he ripped open Garrett's shirt.

Marcus glanced down to see he had been shot in the chest. "Fuck!" He took his shirt and placed it on the wound. "Is there an exit wound?"

Hunter lifted Garrett enough to look. "Yeah."

"Good, he needs to shift." Marcus cursed again, and blood seeped from the exit wound.

"No." Slade ran in with Jill following closely. "I don't want him shifting. Not yet."

"The women are gone," Marcus said to Hunter, their eyes meeting.

"What the fuck is going on?" Jill asked, her eyes wide as she stood by, ready to help Slade if needed. "Where's Janna?"

"They got her," Marcus said, then looked down at his brother. "We have to go after them."

"Go on." Slade cursed as he tried to stop the bleeding.

"Don't let him die," Marcus instructed as he stood, but his blood ran cold when Slade looked up at him with concern. "If he shifts, he'll heal quicker."

"I'll do my best," Slade promised, then nodded. "Go on."

Marcus and Hunter ran out just as Taz ran around the side of the house. "This way."

"Did you see them?" Marcus followed Taz.

"No, but I can track anything." Taz led them into the woods. "And these fuckers are leaving a trail a blind man could find."

Marcus followed him with Hunter, who he knew was raging because he was silent. Hunter was never silent. He would get Roxy and the others back, his brother would survive, and the motherfucker who even dared hurt his family was going to die.

\*\*\*\*\*\*

Roxy did everything in her power to slow them down, even piss them off. The more they focused on her, the less they focused on Janna, who wasn't faring very well with her big belly.

"Didn't think this through, did you?" Roxy complained as they pulled her, Emily, and Janna along. "I mean, a car or van would have made more sense."

"Do you ever shut up?" one of the men said as he jerked the rope around her wrists.

"Sorry, I talk when I'm nervous." Roxy glanced at Emily, who was helping Janna. "But as I was saying, our mates know these woods better than anyone, and I'm sure they heard the gunshot, so I expect them at any time now."

The men laughed, not sharing the joke.

"Did I say something funny?" Roxy asked, not having a good feeling at all.

"Yeah, actually, you did." The one pulling her grinned back at her. "We're smarter than you think, Red."

"Oh, and how's that?" She hated to be called Red.

"Right now, I'd say they are tied up." The man chuckled. "Maybe dead like that big son of a bitch I shot."

Hearing Janna cry out, she glanced over and cringed when Janna fell to her knees. "Hey, slow down with her."

"Shut up." The man jerked Janna up to her feet and began walking again.

"So, what's this all about?" Roxy decided to see if he was in a bragging mood. "Who's calling the shots and what's going to happen to us?"

"It's a paid job." The man jerked the rope. "And for what's to happen to you, I don't know. I was told however many women we can get is more money for us."

"Well, you guys are screwed." Roslyn stepped out of some brush. "Because if you're working with Carl, who is my stepbrother, he doesn't have money."

"Hey!" The man raised a gun, aiming it at Roslyn. "Don't make another move."

Roslyn raised her hands in the air. "I'm no threat to you. Actually, I'm trying to find my stepbrother and figured I'd tag along."

"Do you think I'm stupid?" he sneered, dropping the gun slightly. "And he better fucking pay me."

"Yes, I do, and you just proved it," Roslyn answered, then motioned to Roxy who pulled on the rope that tied her to the man so hard she fell back on her ass.

The gunshot went off, which propelled Roxy back up to her feet. As Roslyn fought the man, Roxy scrambled for the gun. On her scramble there, she saw Emily fighting with the rope while trying to keep the man who held her from getting to the gun.

Finally, Roxy grabbed it, pointed it in the air and fired off a shot. Then she aimed it at the man who Roslyn was beating the shit out of.

"I've got him so stop aiming that fucking gun my way," Roslyn ordered. Then her eyes widened. "Watch out!"

Roxy turned and aimed it at the man who Emily was struggling with. He was making his way toward her. "Stop, or I swear to God I'll shoot you."

A noise to her side startled her, and she aimed that way and fired. Marcus, Hunter, and Taz all dove for the ground with a curse.

"Jesus!" Marcus rolled to his feet, came straight at her and took the gun out of her hand. "Are you hurt?"

"No. I'm fine." Roxy did her best to keep it together. It wasn't time to break down. She saw Hunter beating the shit out of the man who had dared tie a rope on his mate. Taz had already tied up the bastard who had Janna. Marcus, however, stood and cut the ropes off her as he watched Roslyn beat the hell out of the one who'd had control over her.

He dropped the rope then went to Roslyn and tapped her. "It's my turn."

Roslyn stood with a smile and moved out of the way. "I left you some."

Roxy watched as Marcus picked the man up by the hair. "You dare touch my mate?" Marcus sneered. "Did you shoot my brother?"

When the man didn't answer, he turned toward the others. "Who shot my brother?"

They both pointed at the man he held.

"Carl's behind all this? It's got his name all over it. He pays dumbasses who don't know any better, but the thing is, he doesn't have the money to pay, and these stupid asses don't ask for it up front." Roslyn shook her head in disgust.

"He will die soon," Marcus said, still staring at the bastard in his grip. Marcus then punched him in the face with a wicked smile. "Unfortunately, my brother, who will survive, has dibs on you." He reached down, grabbed the rope and wrapped it tightly around the man's neck.

"You want me to take him?" Roslyn asked with a wicked smile of her own. "He's a pussy. I can handle him."

Marcus tossed her the rope. "Make sure it's a torturous walk through the woods."

"Hey, we got a problem." Taz frowned, looking down at Janna before looking back up. "I think her water just broke."

# Chapter 20

Marcus rushed to Janna and cursed. Her face was scrunched with pain. "Ah shit." Marcus looked around. He knew it was too early and didn't know what the fuck he was going to do to get her out of there.

Roslyn hurried over and knocked him out of the way. She put her hand on Janna's stomach. "How far along are you?"

When Janna didn't answer because she was biting her lip in pain, Roxy stepped up. "Not far enough."

"Well, that depends," Roslyn said, looking at the ground underneath her. "She's a shifter. We have different term lengths, but she's carrying twins, isn't she?"

"Yes," Marcus replied, before turning and glancing up the hill, ready for battle. His hearing was superb and he was alert, but it was only Dell who rushed toward them.

"We need to get her the hell out of here, that's for sure." Roslyn stood, then reached for her phone when it dinged. Looking down, she cursed long and loud. She tossed it to Marcus. "Will you please kill the son of a bitch for me? I would, but I think I need to stay with the pregnant one just in case she decides to drop these babies in the woods."

Janna cursed as she narrowed her eyes at Roslyn.

"Just kidding." Roslyn smiled at her and patted her hand.

"I need to get back to Garrett," Janna cried, her eyes looking up to Dell. "Is he okay?"

"Slade's with him," Dell said, his eyes shifting away, giving no more information, which said a lot. He looked at Marcus. "Leda is missing."

"What?" Taz became alert, his eyes going to Dell.

"Fuck!" Marcus looked at the text that said: **Tell them to find me if they can**, and had a picture of Leda.

What the fuck? How in the hell could all this shit go down at once? His brother fucking shot, Janna about ready to give birth to twins in the woods, his mate kidnapped, and now the motherfucker who started it all had Leda and was playing "find me if you can" games. Oh, and God forbid he forget he and Hunter walking into a fucking trap. What in the hell was he supposed to do? Go after Leda, stay with Roxy, or run to his brother's side?

"You need to find Leda." Roxy walked up to him, pulling his attention from the phone to her, and making the decision for him. "I'm fine. Janna and your brother will be fine. I'm heading there now and will stay by their sides until you get back. But you must go and you know it. Leda's in danger."

Son of a bitch. He didn't know what he did in his lifetime to deserve a woman like Roxy Patel, but he was one lucky bastard. He pulled her to him and kissed her hard. "I fucking love you," he whispered.

"And I fucking love you," she whispered back. "Now go, and yes, before you ask, I'm fine. I'm pretty damn tough. And I'm sorry about shooting at you."

"Yeah, about that." Marcus narrowed his eyes at her. "Definitely gun lessons for you."

"Let me see that." Taz took the phone, his eyes narrowing as he studied the picture. "I know where this is."

"Where?" Marcus looked down at the picture, trying to see what Taz was seeing.

"East of here, near the hidden waterfalls." Taz pointed to the tree Leda was tied up to. "I know that tree."

"How in the hell?" Marcus was impressed, but he was right. He also knew that spot, but never would have figured it out.

"I'm not only one of the best trackers, but I also memorize territory. I've run these lands for a long time." Taz glanced back at Janna. "I can go alone if you need me to."

"No." Marcus handed Roslyn back her phone, but she wouldn't take it.

"Keep it. The dumbass might text something you need to know." Roslyn unlocked the phone so it wouldn't lock again. "If it does lock, the passcode is 1440."

Marcus nodded and stuck the phone in his pocket. "Dell, can you get the women back safely?"

"I don't know," Hunter intervened, not looking certain. "How do we know if that asshole at Jonah's and these three idiots are the only ones around here?"

"Damn. True." Marcus turned and looked at the asshole who appeared the most scared. He walked over and picked him up by the throat. "How many are working for him? If you lie to me, you have no chance in hell of living through this."

"This is it," the man cried out. "I swear it. If you got Perry, then that's all of us."

"I got it." Dell looked at the man in disgust. "Go on."

Dell reached down and with Roslyn's help, lifted Janna carefully into his arms. Hunter kissed Emily, who hugged him tightly. Marcus was ready to hug Roxy when Jonah, Josh, and Devon came down the hill.

"Slade's transferring Garrett to the hospital," Jonah said, his eyes taking in everything. "He said he's lost a lot of blood and needs a transfusion."

"Shit." Marcus frowned. "He can't have human blood."

"He's not. Every shifter in town is going to the hospital to give theirs." Jonah glanced at Janna, who was listening to everything he said. "He woke for just a minute asking for you. We told him you were fine and that calmed him."

"I need to get to him," Janna said weakly, and Dell began to head up the hill.

"I'll get you there." Dell and Roslyn took off with Janna. Emily followed closely.

"Can you guys handle them?" Marcus nodded behind him. "The bastard has Leda, but we know where he is."

"I'm going with you." Devon stepped up, but Taz blocked him.

"No, you're not," Taz growled, then looked at Marcus.

"Who the fuck do you think you are?" Devon went to shove Taz, but Taz was too quick and had Devon on the ground, his face plastered in the dirt. "Stay away from Leda."

Marcus cursed. "Come the fuck on." He pulled Taz off Devon. "We don't have time for this shit. Fight over her later. Right now I need Taz with me, and I need you to help Jonah and Josh get the women out of here safely and these assholes locked up until we get back."

Devon cursed but didn't argue. He grabbed one of the men and headed up the hill, giving Taz a deadly look as he passed.

"Go on, Roxy." He kissed her. "I'll be back soon."

"Promise?" She hugged his neck. "I'll be really mad if you're not."

"Promise. Go on." He nudged her toward the hill. "Catch up with Emily."

Roxy nodded and turned to leave. Marcus watched them all go until they disappeared, then turned toward Taz and Hunter. "You ready?"

"Yeah, let's get this fucker." Hunter took off first, then Taz. Marcus took one last look up the hill and then chased after them. They decided against shifting for now, at least until they knew what they were running toward. Plus, fighting naked sucked, and none of them had extra clothes stashed close to that area.

Marcus calmed his mind as they ran. He needed to get his thoughts straight before this confrontation. They sped past the trees, managing the jumps with ease. He was also impressed with Taz, who kept up, and he was right. The guy knew these woods as well as them, if not better. He noticed Hunter had fallen back to give Taz the lead. Marcus decided to do the same and trust him.

After about twenty minutes, Taz slowed, holding up his hand. That was when Marcus smelled the smoke from a wood fire. Carl was either stupid, or he didn't give a shit. Most would know that a wood fire would give the person's whereabouts away, but then again, he offered the challenge of finding him, and they'd accepted.

"There's a ledge just above those trees. If one of you goes that way, we can gain the element of surprise from above." Taz glanced toward that area before looking back at Marcus.

"How old are you?" Marcus cocked his eyebrow at him.

"Twenty-one, sir." Taz frowned. "Why?"

"Because if you keep this up, you will definitely earn your spot in the higher ranks." Marcus gave him a nod, then looked at Hunter. "You take the ridge. Me and Taz will come in on opposite sides."

Hunter took off the way Taz directed him to go. Then Marcus and Taz took off in opposite directions. Slowing, Marcus took his time, his ears straining for sound. He heard two men arguing in the distance. Glancing around, he noticed what looked like a trail. At least he hoped that was what it was since he couldn't see shit through all the brush. Sure enough, there was an opening, but he stopped, wanting to make sure Hunter was in place first.

Backing up, he saw Hunter looking down at him. He held up two fingers indicating two men. Then he positioned his hand like a gun, then lifted two fingers, indicating that both men were armed. He nodded but waited as he looked to his left and then gave a thumbs-up, telling him Taz was in place.

Marcus eased himself closer. His blood boiled at what he heard, but he refrained from rushing in. He didn't need to get shot. He knew Leda was going to be close by, and he didn't want any bullets flying her way.

Finding a bare spot in the brush along the trail, he stepped inside and looked out. Carl stood next to a fire. Another man argued with him, pointing toward Leda, whose shirt was torn and hanging off her. One breast was almost bare, and she was shivering. They had her tied up tight so she couldn't shift.

"If you don't have my money, then I'm taking her." The other man's voice rose in anger. "I told them you weren't going to pay."

"The job isn't done yet," Carl said with a growl. "And I honestly don't give a shit what you do with her after I kill that asshole. I've got his redheaded bitch, so I know he'll be coming after her."

If he only knew…. Marcus's smile grew wicked. He was going to enjoy fucking this guy up.

"And about that." The man looked around, making Marcus back deeper into the shadows. "Shouldn't they be here by now?"

"Give them time." Carl snorted. "My plan was foolproof."

"Well, I hope to fuck so because you definitely had some fools on this job," the man spat, then turned toward Leda. "Damn, she is fine-looking. How old did you say you were, baby?" He walked over and knelt in front of Leda, moving her shirt away, baring her breast.

Marcus's eyes narrowed, but he kept his cool. He was actually in a really bad spot. If he jumped out and Carl shot toward him, he could hit Leda.

"Answer me." The man grabbed her face, squeezing it.

"Fuck you," Leda hissed, and Marcus cringed, wishing she would tone it down, but deep inside, he was damn proud of her for not taking any shit. Then he heard her spit.

The sound of a slap had him moving, but he stopped when he heard Taz.

"You touch her again and I'll kill you slowly." Marcus watched as Taz walked into the open as plain as day.

"Dammit!" Marcus cursed when he saw the gun raised at Taz, but before he could make a move, Taz moved with lightning speed and dropped the guy with a knife in the throat. "Holy fuck!"

Marcus took off, and Hunter jumped from the ledge just as Carl raised his gun toward Taz. Marcus got to him first and took him down. They rolled, but Marcus was much stronger. He took his hand and continued to smash it on the ground until the gun released. Hunter swooped in and took control of it.

Feeling around, he made sure Carl didn't have another gun. Then he climbed off him. "You wanted me. Here I am, motherfucker." Marcus took a step back and waved toward him. "You have no clue who you're fucking with."

Carl eased his way backward, his hands outstretched. "I wasn't going to hurt her." He glanced to where Taz was cutting Leda loose. "I was just ensuring that—"

"Honestly, I don't give two fucks. You're dead, no matter what you say." Marcus stalked toward him. He knew the bastard was easing his way toward the knife sticking out of the other man's throat, and Marcus wished he would grab it. "Go ahead. I'll let you get the knife, but it's not going to save you."

Surprise and fear flashed in Carl's eyes, but he ran to the dead man and grabbed the knife, jerking it to free it from the dead man's neck.

"Damn, Taz." Hunter laughed. "You buried that deep in the son of a bitch's throat, didn't you?"

Finally, Carl got the knife free and held it up in front of him. "Don't come any closer."

"Jesus, it's about time you got that knife out. I was getting bored as fuck." Hunter yawned and stretched. "Go ahead and kill the son of a bitch, Marcus. I'm hungry."

Marcus grinned. Hunter always could make a killing entertaining. "You had my brother shot, you put the lives of not only my mate, but my brothers' mates in danger, you kidnapped a member of our pack and all because of what?"

"Garrett's been shot?" Leda cried out, but Marcus ignored her.

"Answer me!" he roared. "Is it because I bested you after you tried to attack my mate?"

"Yes," Carl admitted, his eyes shifting between him and Hunter. "You don't remember me, do you?"

"No, I don't." Marcus realized at that moment shit was probably going to get real.

"Your brother killed my father," Carl hissed with bitterness. "Jasper Simone was my father. I was at the reaping when your redheaded bitch was to be sacrificed."

"Holy shit! No, wait. Nope, I don't remember you." Hunter stood, his eyes narrowed. "And the saying 'the apple doesn't fall far from the tree' seems to make sense now. Hey, wait a minute. His son's name was Evan and didn't we kill him too? Damn, dude, we fucked up your family. Guess they shouldn't have been fucking losers."

"Fuck you! Evan was my stepbrother," Carl spat toward Hunter.

"Damn, Jasper got around." Hunter cocked his eyebrow. "And is Jasper Ross's dad too?"

"No, asshole. Same mom, different dad," Carl said, then frowned. "Why the fuck am I even explaining this to you?"

"I just got one of those faces you want to tell everything to," Hunter replied in his smartass tone.

"When I heard you were recruiting, I decided to join up, but then your stupid slut ruined all that. So if I do die today, I know I have avenged my father, the man your brother killed." Carl ignored Hunter, his little speech directed toward Marcus.

"Well, guess what, fucker?" Marcus stalked toward him, then knocked the knife he threw at him away. He stopped close to Carl's face. "You failed because the men you hired failed. My brother is alive and well, but you... will die just like your piece-of-shit father did."

Marcus punched him in the throat and enjoyed watching him fight to breathe. He snatched his hair, lifting his head back up. "And know, you're dying as the biggest pussy I've ever seen." Marcus head butted him and welcomed the pain. It made him alert to what was going on. "Anyone who has to hire people to kill for their revenge doesn't even deserve the slow death I wanted to give you."

Carl was still trying to breathe as he grabbed at his throat. Marcus looked toward Taz, who threw him a knife. He caught it and held it up to Carl's face. "Any last words?" Marcus quickly sliced his throat without waiting to hear them. "Tough, asshole. Rot in hell." He dropped Carl to the ground.

He looked toward Leda who was wearing Taz's shirt. "You okay?"

"Yeah." Leda nodded. "I'm good. Thanks."

"Jasper fucking Simone." Hunter shook his head. "Isn't that a blast from the past?"

"Come on." Marcus glanced around, knowing the animals would take care of the bodies. "Put that fire out and let's go. Can you run?" he asked Leda.

"Of course." Leda nodded as she stood and stretched her legs. "Just give me a second. Been in that position too long."

"I'll hang with her until she gets her speed," Taz offered, helping Hunter put out the fire. "I know you guys want to get back to your brother."

"Is he going to be okay?" Leda asked, her eyes filling with tears.

"I don't know." Marcus looked back at Hunter. "You ready?"

"Let's go." They all took off, not giving the dead a second glance.

# Chapter 21

"What in the hell are you doing in there?" Marcus called out, then knocked on the bathroom door. "We're going to be late."

"Hold on a minute," Roxy called back. "Can't a girl have some privacy?"

"No, she can't." Marcus grinned, leaning against the wall near the bathroom. His eyes roamed the room, seeing all the special touches Roxy had put into their home, and it made him feel almost emotional. After nearly losing his brother, his eyes had been opened more than they ever had. He had so much to lose and it scared him. Nothing ever had scared him more than losing family or his mate.

Finally, the door opened and Roxy came out closing the door behind her. Her face looked flushed, her eyes bright like she had been crying.

"Jeez-o-pete, Mr. Impatient," Roxy teased. "I'm ready to go."

"What's wrong?" Marcus became instantly alert. He knew her better than he knew himself, and something was wrong.

"Nothing." Roxy tried to pass him, but he stopped her.

"Do not lie to me, Roxy," Marcus warned with a frown. "Your face is flushed, and it looks like you've been crying."

"I'm flushed because you're rushing me," Roxy countered. "And I've not been crying. Now can we please go? I want to be there before the babies come home. You're always making us late."

"What?" Marcus's head shot back, his eyes widened. "You're the one who makes us late. I hate being late."

Roxy laughed as she hurried down the steps. She grabbed the gifts off the table and headed for the door. "Come on, slow poke."

"I'll give you a slow poke." He grabbed the keys and swatted her ass.

The drive was quick, but he still noticed something was off with Roxy. She wasn't her talkative self on the short drive to Garrett's. He put it in the back of his mind but would get the truth out of her once they got back home. He pulled up to Garrett's, and Roxy cursed.

"Shit, they beat us here." Roxy sighed and hurried out of the car.

"Your fault," Marcus teased, which gained him a glare.

He followed her inside, and the house was full of activity. Marcus couldn't help but glance at the kitchen floor that only weeks before was soaked with his brother's blood. He found Garrett proudly standing over Janna, with one of the babies in his arms. Garrett looked up, and their eyes met. Marcus gave him a wave and a nod.

Without Slade, his brother probably would have bled to death on this floor. The gunshot wound itself wasn't life threatening, meaning it didn't cause any internal damage. It was the blood loss that had been the concern, but the town of shifters showed up at the hospital and gave their blood. Something he would never be able to repay them for. He had shown up at the hospital, and after checking on everyone, he had then headed down to give blood along with Hunter. There was a line. It was something he would never forget. Once Garrett received the transfusion, and he was strong enough, he shifted. Within no time, he'd healed enough to go to Janna.

Marcus watched Roxy make her way up to the babies. Janna looked a hundred percent better. She had been in premature labor in the woods. Once Dell got her to the hospital, they gave her something to try to slow it down. Slade hadn't been sure if the babies were strong enough to come into the world. If it had been just one, it would have been fine since a shifter's pregnancy term is half of a human's. But with twins, even a few weeks early could be devastating.

Roxy waved him over as she held one of the babies. "Isn't she just adorable?" She ran her finger down the baby's soft, round cheek. "Say hi to your Uncle Marcus."

Marcus smiled and touched the baby's hand. Shifters liked to mate. They usually had big families, and he knew the urge to mate with Roxy after seeing the baby was normal. His makeup was saying it was time. He just hoped Roxy was ready.

"Can I have everyone's attention?" Garrett called out, quieting everyone. "We held off telling anyone the names we picked out until we were all together."

Janna stood next to Garrett and took the baby girl from Roxy. "This is Maria Huntress Foster."

"Well, I'll be damned," Hunter said, looking a little emotional. "She'll be spoiled rotten with a name like that."

"A hellion more like it," someone else called out.

Hunter looked offended at first but then grinned. "Yeah, definitely a hellion."

Everyone laughed until Garrett held up the other baby. "And this little guy is Maximus Marcus Foster."

Marcus grinned proudly. "I'm honored and will teach the little guy everything I know."

"God help us!" someone yelled as others agreed.

"Congratulations." Roxy kissed his cheek. "Uncle Marcus."

"Do you have a minute?" Garrett walked up to them. "Can I borrow your mate?"

"Of course, as long as I can borrow one of those cuties." Roxy grinned then headed toward the babies.

"How you feeling?" Marcus followed Garrett outside where Hunter was obviously waiting for them. "Where's Slade and Jill? I thought they'd be here."

"Feeling real good, never better in fact, and they got called back," Garrett replied. "They were hoping to stay until tomorrow, but something came up and they had to leave."

Marcus watched Garrett closely and knew something big was about to happen. Garrett usually said what was on his mind without hesitation, but he could tell he was choosing his words.

"I wanted to thank you both for what you did for Janna and me. If it wasn't for you, I probably would have lost my life, my mate, and my babies, as well as Leda. I can never repay you for that."

"You'll never have to repay us for that," Marcus said, and Hunter agreed. "It's the shifter way. We take care of ours."

Garrett nodded, then glanced out over the yard. "I'm stepping down," he blurted before looking at each of them.

"What?" Hunter frowned. "No, wait. What?"

"It's not just me anymore. Janna doesn't even know. But I am stepping down as alpha." Garrett held his hand out before Hunter could say anything else. "I can't put my family in this kind of danger

189

anymore. I've been thinking this for a while, but this shit like Jasper Simone's son coming back is a wake-up call. There'll be others out there seeking revenge because I killed someone. It's different when I take that chance, but it's selfish to have my family in harm's way when they don't have to be. The last thing I'll do before I step down is take care of the motherfucker who shot me. The others can be dealt with however the new alpha sees fit."

"Well fuck!" Hunter cursed, looking conflicted. "I mean, I understand, but damn, man. This sucks."

"What do you say, Marcus?" Garrett looked him directly in the eye.

"Before Roxy, I would have given you hell, but I understand. Now you have babies and well, yeah, it sucks because you're one hell of an alpha to our pack, but I get it and I support you."

"Thank you." Garrett nodded. "That means a lot. I'm offering you both the position. If you both want it, then you have to fight for it. I expect an answer soon. I want this done as soon as possible. If neither of you wants it, I'm going to offer it to Dell."

Marcus took it all in. He wouldn't really say he was surprised by Garrett's decision, but it was a reality check in the kind of life they lived.

"Any one of you will make a great alpha. I wanted you to know first and will wait until you make your decision before I approach Dell," Garrett said, then clapped Hunter on the back. "Now come on, and let's enjoy the rest of the day with family and friends."

Marcus smiled and followed them in, but his mood took a drastic turn. It wasn't as festive as it was before. His eyes met Roxy's questioning gaze, but he gave her a smile of reassurance. He didn't want her to worry.

******

Roxy knew something was wrong as soon as Hunter, Garrett, and Marcus came back inside. She also knew Marcus's smile was as fake as hell. Clare had walked up to see the babies, and they began talking, but she wasn't focused. Looking around, she didn't see Marcus anywhere.

"Hey!" Emily called out, waving her over. "Can you help me put out the food?"

Roxy agreed, but in truth, she wanted to find Marcus. Clare came over to help, and in no time, the food was out, and people were filling their plates. Every time she went to find Marcus, someone stopped her to talk or she needed to help with something.

Finally, she got away and searched and searched. Walking outside, she spotted him leaning against the old wooden fence in the side yard. After heading down the steps, she crossed the grass. "Hey, I've been looking everywhere for you." She glided into his arms. "You okay?"

"Yeah, fine." He smiled down at her then hugged her close, putting his chin on her head.

"Well, we're both lying to each other," Roxy said, and he pulled away from her.

"I knew something was wrong." He frowned down at her. "What is it?"

"You first." Roxy stared up at him. "Please."

"You know I can't deny you when you say please so sweetly like that." Marcus sighed and then cursed.

"I know." She chuckled. "That's why I do it."

"Garrett's stepping down as alpha," Marcus said, then looked toward the house. "He's offered the position to me or Hunter."

"Why's he stepping down?" Roxy asked. She didn't really understand the whole alpha thing, but knew it was a big deal, and Marcus seemed truly upset.

"Because of family." Marcus looked back at her. "Being alpha brings not only a lot of responsibility but danger as well. When you have a family, they're at risk."

"Oh," Roxy replied. Her stomach flipped and dipped. "And what do you want to do?"

"I don't know. It's a big decision, and I want to make the right one for us, for the pack, and for Garrett." Marcus tipped her chin up, looking into her eyes. "I'm sorry, this just has my mind whirling like crazy."

"Whatever you decide, know that I'm behind you," Roxy assured him and meant it. She was in this for the long haul.

"Thank you." Marcus leaned down, kissing her softly.

"But I think I really need to tell you something before you make your decision." Roxy backed away from him so she could watch his reaction.

"What?" Marcus reached for her, but she backed further way. "Why are you backing away from me?"

"Because I want to see your expression when I tell you that I'm pregnant," Roxy said, then cringed looking at him, waiting.

Marcus opened his mouth, then shut it. Barely a second later, a large grin spread across his face. "You're sure?"

"That's why I was in the bathroom so long," Roxy said, still watching him closely. "And if four positive tests mean sure, then yeah, I'm pretty sure."

"Yes!" Marcus shouted and grabbed her, picking her up in the air. "Fuck yes!"

"So, I take it you're happy." Roxy laughed as he slowly lowered her so he could kiss her, but her feet still didn't touch the ground.

"Hell yes, I'm happy." Marcus finally put her on the ground. He hugged her close. "Thank you."

"For being pregnant?" Roxy grinned against his chest.

"Yes, thank you for being pregnant and coming into my life." He kissed her again.

"Well, you needed to know for when you make your decision about the alpha stuff." Roxy frowned. "Sorry, I don't really understand the whole alpha thing, but I trust whatever decision you make."

"Let's not talk about that right now." Marcus laughed, then grabbed her hand. "I want to tell everyone I'm going to be a dad."

"Whoa, hold on there." Roxy pulled him back. "We can't do that here at Garrett and Janna's party."

"The hell we can't." Marcus tugged her toward the house. Once inside, he stood in the middle of the room and yelled, "I'm going to be a fucking dad!"

"Oh, damn!" Hunter shouted in fake shock. "Let's pray it's not a girl!"

Everyone laughed and started to congratulate them, but Marcus held up his hand and everyone became silent. He turned to Garrett and Janna, who both wore large grins. "I don't want to steal your thunder—"

"Too late for that." Hunter snorted, then laughed when Marcus glared at him.

"But—" He turned to Roxy and knelt on the ground. "I did this once, but now I want to do it in front of my family and friends so no one can question my feelings for you."

"Marcus, you don't have—" Roxy started to say, but tears choked her.

"Hell yes, he does." Clare cut her off, excitement in her voice.

"Roxy Patel, will you marry me?" Marcus held a small box with a simple single stone diamond ring inside.

"Yes, I will marry you," Roxy whispered, then held out her hand and still on her ring finger was the twig ring that he proposed with in the woods. He went to remove it, but she snatched her hand back. "Don't you dare."

"She's already bossing him around." Hunter sighed, then grunted when Emily elbowed him in the stomach.

Marcus slipped the ring on her finger; it butted up against the other. He stood in front of her. The seriousness in his eyes had her sighing, crying, and wanting nothing more than to be alone with him.

"I've waited my whole life for you." Marcus leaned down, kissing her, then took her in his arms.

"I know exactly what you mean." Roxy held him close and felt like she had finally come home.

The cheers were loud as they were surrounded, everyone congratulating them. She was a little embarrassed by all the attention, but seeing the joy on Marcus's face, she smiled. This definitely must be the shifter way.

Made in the USA
Lexington, KY
25 May 2017